2-93

GUB-GUB'S BOOK

HUGH LOFTING

GUB-GUB'S BOOK

An Encyclopaedia of Food in Twenty Volumes

Note: Professor Gub-Gub announces that owing to the high cost of living, the other nineteen volumes of this great work have been temporarily postponed

SIMON & SCHUSTER BOOKS FOR YOUNG READERS
PUBLISHED BY SIMON & SCHUSTER
NEW YORK·LONDON·TORONTO·SYDNEY·TOKYO·SINGAPORE

SIMON & SCHUSTER BOOKS FOR YOUNG READERS
Simon & Schuster Building, Rockefeller Center
1230 Avenue of the Americas, New York, New York 10020
Copyright © 1932 by Hugh Lofting
Copyright © renewed 1960 by Josephine Lofting
Additional illustrations copyright © 1992 by Christopher Lofting
SIMON & SCHUSTER BOOKS FOR YOUNG READERS
is a trademark of Simon & Schuster.
Designed by Vicki Kalajian
Manufactured in the United States of America.

10 9 8 7 6 5 4 3 2 1

LIBRARY OF CONGRESS CATALOGING-IN-PUBLICATION DATA
Lofting, Hugh, 1886–1947. Gub-Gub's book / by Hugh Lofting.
p. cm. Summary: On a succession of evenings, the animals settle into
Doctor Dolittle's kitchen to hear Gub-Gub the pig
read parts of his book on food.
[1. Food—Fiction. 2. Animals—Fiction. 3. Fantasy.]
I. Title. PZ7.L827Gu 1992 [Fic]—dc20 91–47563
ISBN: 0–671–78355–6 CIP AC

To *"Dutchie"*
Nora van Leeuwen of the Dutchoven
that greatest of artists in cooking
Gub-Gub dedicates with deep respect
this book

CONTENTS

INTRODUCTION

TOMMY STUBBINS, THE SON OF JACOB STUBBINS,
COBBLER OF PUDDLEBY-ON-THE-MARSH,
EXPLAINS SOME THINGS ABOUT THIS BOOK
AND GUB-GUB THE PIG

I never thought that I would find a book about Gub-Gub a more difficult task than the books I have written about Doctor Dolittle. Yet this is true.

With the Doctor, although the work of being his secretary often kept me up very late at night, taking notes full of arithmetic and science, there was this to make it easier: I nearly always had the great man himself there, to ask questions of, if I should get stuck.

But with Gub-Gub it was difficult. There wasn't much arithmetic or deep science about what he wanted written; but he was very little help to me when we got to a difficult place. Whenever there was any question or doubt, it was I who had to do most of the deciding. John Dolittle was himself a very good author with a lot of experience; while Gub-Gub —although he wanted everyone to think him the greatest author in the world—had no experience at all.

Yet for whatever faults this book may have, Gub-Gub must not be held entirely to blame. Perhaps I am by no means the best person for the work. Maybe I am not what is called a good editor, that is, one who is clever at arranging, and putting in good, understandable words, the writings and sayings of others. But at the time that this was written there were very few people besides the Doctor and me who could understand animal languages. Someday, no doubt, there will be many more.

John Dolittle himself, of course, could have done much better; and I had hoped that he would undertake the work. Gub-Gub had asked me to go and speak to him about it. But Dab-Dab the duck overheard our talk. And although she was only a duck, she took wonderfully good care of the Doctor and his home.

"Tommy Stubbins," said she to me—severely—"if you bother John Dolittle with putting that silly pig's nonsense-scribble into human writing, there is going to be trouble. You know very well the poor man is far too busy with really important matters to fuss around with a stupid hog's gabblings about food."

"Oh, but, Dab-Dab," I said, "eating and food are very important to the human race too, after all. I have looked over what Gub-Gub has written in pig language, and much of it is quite good—and quite amusing."

"That's just it, Tommy," said she, ruffling her feathers. "He has told me some of the things he wants to have put in his book. He is trying to be funny most of the time. Eating is not a matter to be played with and joked about. It is a serious subject."

"Oh, well now, Dab-Dab," said I, "I'm not so sure. Eating should be a jolly business. I admit it's serious enough when you're starving. But you yourself take life too seriously altogether."

"Well," said she, shrugging her wings, "I have plenty of cause to—with this family. But the Doctor's too busy. There are no two ways about that. If Gub-Gub's book must be put into English, why don't you do it yourself, Tommy?"

After thinking this over, I decided the housekeeper was right. Poor John Dolittle, with all his work in doctoring the creatures that flocked to his doors morning, noon, and night—together with the many books he was writing on animal medicine and natural history—certainly had no time to spare.

And so that was how I came to take on the job myself.

Gub-Gub was delighted, when I told him, to know that his work, on which he had labored so long, was at last going to be published, printed on a real printing press, and sold in the bookshops.

He was a little disappointed when I told him I feared I could not use his own drawings as illustrations. I would have liked to. But—well—Gub-Gub's pictures were distinctly piggy pictures, and I doubted if any printer could have printed them. Gub-Gub was no ordinary artist. He did not often use pencil or ink or paint. He liked much better to do his illustration in mud, drawn on the stable walls. He even painted one picture (the portrait of the "Picnic King") in strawberry jam and mint jelly. He said that no paint or chalks, nothing, could give him just the beautiful green he needed, except mint jelly. I told him I was sorry, but I thought perhaps it would make things easier for the printers if I did the pictures and left out the mint jelly.

I cannot say that I think my own illustrations nearly as striking and unusual as Gub-Gub's. But at least this much must be said of them: I have tried my hardest to carry out Gub-Gub's wishes in every picture. The pig watched over my shoulder while I did them, grunting out remarks and orders until they looked exactly the way he wanted them to be.

But alas! When I came to go over what he had written (in the Dolittle Pig Alphabet) I found I had a much bigger task to deal with than I had reckoned on. To begin with, the pages were very hard to read. Turning written Piggish into English is not easy at best. The spoken, or grunted, language is fairly simple—if you have had plenty of practice. But Gub-Gub, although he had had many lessons from the Doctor in writing Pig signs in copybooks, was a very untidy author. The pages were full of blots—large, messy blots. Many of these were caused by his eating ripe tomatoes when he was at work—tomatoes gave him ideas, he said. And of course the juice of the tomatoes was always running down onto the paper and getting mixed up with the ink.

And, oh, what a lot he had written, to be sure! He

used wrapping paper instead of ordinary writing paper. He hated to write in what he called a small, finicky hand. And one whole attic in the Doctor's house was filled, from floor to ceiling, with sheets and sheets of brown paper a yard square and all covered with his bold, untidy handwriting—foot-writing was what Dab-Dab called it.

Some people who read this will remember that the pig, when he first spoke to the Doctor's animal family about his book on the art of eating, said he was going to call it, *A Short Encyclopaedia of Food—In Twenty Volumes*. But also, we must not forget, Gub-Gub knew so much about food that twenty volumes would seem by no means long to one as learned in the art of feeding as he was.

And so I had to give him a second disappointment when I told him I would have to cut it down in order that we could print a book about the ordinary size that most books are.

More than that, when I had sorted out from the great mass of his writings those parts which I thought people—human readers—would like best, I saw it would help a lot if I added something about how he collected his information for the book, and, well, a few other little things that will be read and understood later on.

INTRODUCTION

I do not mean that any of Gub-Gub's book is not strictly his own. It is only that I had to change the form as well as the length of it. It took me a long time to think of this best form or arrangement. And this was how I at last decided:

The pig author was in the habit of reading what he had written to anyone who would listen to him. As soon as he got a new chapter finished, he would try it out on the other animals of the Doctor's household. He nearly always did it in the evening, when the animals usually clustered round the fire before going to bed. It became almost a regular thing to have the whole family—Jip the dog, Too-Too the owl, Dab-Dab the duck, Cheapside the London sparrow, the White Mouse, and sometimes myself—gather in that comfortable kitchen of the Doctor's after supper while Gub-Gub sat at the table and read to us from his sheets of wrapping paper. He often also lectured to us, explaining his book as he went along. He called it "author's readings."

The other animals, of course, gave their opinions, saying which parts they liked and which parts they didn't like—sometimes not very politely. A good deal of what they had to say, for and against, struck me as being important and worth putting into the book. The author's readings, however, spread over many weeks — some months, in fact. Therefore, I found that again I had to cut down. And, as will be seen, in the form in which I did give the book to the printers I have taken ten of these evening gatherings, or readings, and made them into chapters. In each of them I have set down everything as it happened and every word as it was said, whether it came from Gub-Gub himself or from those who were listening to him.

And so we will begin with —

THE FIRST EVENING

"**M**y-Goodness-Gracious-Mary-Agnes!" cried Dab-Dab, flouncing into the room. She threw down a tray with a great clatter upon the table. "That pig will be the death of me yet."

"Why?" asked Jip. "What has he done now?"

"What has he done?" squawked the duck. "I thought the end of my patience was reached when he started calling himself *Doctor* Gub-Gub, D.S.D., but—"

"What does D.S.D. mean?" asked the White Mouse.

"Doctor of Salad Dressings, if you please," snorted Dab-Dab. "That was bad enough. But now he has gotten hold of a pair of John Dolittle's spectacles. There's no glass in them—just the tortoiseshell frames. And he's wearing them. Thinks they make

him look like an author. At this moment he's traipsing around the house with those spectacles on his
snout, spouting passages from his own silly book."

"Tee-hee-hee!" tittered the White Mouse. "What a
picture! But you know, Dab-Dab, I think his book
ought to be lots of fun. An encyclopaedia of food. I've
no idea what *encyclopaedia* means, but it sounds like
something awfully good to eat—something that
would last a long time too. I do hope Gub-Gub has
plenty about cheeses in his book."

"Oh, you *would* like your books to be cheesy,"
growled Jip. He was lying on the hearth, his nose
between his paws stretched out toward the fire, his
eyes shut. Anyone would think he was asleep, but this
was only his favorite way of listening to the conversa-
tion after supper, and he never missed a thing.

"Huh! And you would like your books to be beefy, I
suppose," smirked the White Mouse, turning up his
pink nose.

Too-Too the owl, the great mathematician, was
seated on the back of my chair, still and quiet as the
furniture itself.

"That pig, Gub-Gub," he said presently in a
thoughtful voice, "reminds me of a boy I knew once.
A small boy with a large appetite—lived on a farm
where I had a nest in the barn. One day a visitor asked

him what was his favorite sport. 'Eating,' he answered. 'Well, but what is your favorite outdoor sport?' asked the visitor. 'Eating outdoors,' said the boy.''

"Yes, that sounds like our Gubby, all right," chirped Cheapside the London sparrow. He hopped up onto the table and began his usual job of helping Dab-Dab to clear away by picking up the crumbs on the tablecloth.

"Tell me, Tommy," he said, " 'ow does our Perfesser Bacon manage about 'is spellin'?"

"He doesn't, Cheapside," said I. "You see, the Dolittle Pig Alphabet is made up of signs, not letters. Each sign stands for a word, sometimes for a whole sentence."

"Huh! Something like Chinese?"

"Yes," I said, "something like it—only much simpler."

"It would have to be that indeed," said Dab-Dab. "The simpleton! He's forever nosing into the Doctor's books about gardening and cooking. But of course he isn't reading really—just pretending. It's my opinion that pig couldn't spell the word *ham*—not if you promised him a seven-course meal."

"Just the same," chuckled Polynesia the parrot from the top of the grandfather clock, "it is wonderful how much information he has managed to collect for his book."

Chee-Chee the monkey slid across the floor and threw another log on the fire.

"Yes," he said, "and he doesn't get it all from books. He pesters me all the time to tell him about the African jungle fruits, and the vegetables too—like yams and wild mangoes, palm kernels, dates, ground nuts, and whatnot."

"Well, you're all going to get a dose of him very soon, I fancy," muttered Dab-Dab. "When I was washing the dishes just now, he passed through the pantry, and he said something about giving us an author's reading tonight. So those who would like to go to bed had better go—oh, goodness! Here he comes."

There was a knock upon the door. Gub-Gub's only difficulty in getting about the house was the door-knobs. He had to use both his front trotters to turn them, and he always knocked when he could get any-one else to let him in.

"It's he, sure enough," giggled the White Mouse.

I rose and pulled the door wide. In the opening stood a strange figure: Gub-Gub as an author. Under one arm he carried a large, untidy bundle of papers; behind his ear there was an enormous quill pen; upon

"In the opening stood a strange figure"

his nose there was a pair of tortoiseshell spectacle frames; and upon his face there was a look of great weariness.

"Dear, dear!" he sighed. "No one has any idea how fatigued I am."

"Fat you may be," snorted Dab-Dab. "But what should make you *fat*igued?"

"Research," the great author groaned. "Untiring, endless research."

"Where did you do your research," asked Jip, "in the strawberry bed?"

"What is research?" asked the White Mouse.

Gub-Gub pulled a chair up to the table beside my own and sat down. Then he wiped his spectacles carefully—although they hadn't any glass in them— upon the tablecloth and put them back on his nose. "Research?" said he. "Well—er—research is—er— bibliography."

"And what is bibliography?" the White Mouse asked in a meek voice.

"Oh, you go to libraries and you read their books. Then you know what to put in your own."

"Ah, I see. Just copying," snickered the White Mouse.

"Not at all," said Gub-Gub with an annoyed look on his face. "It isn't copying at all. It's very hard to describe. There are some things in the life of a great writer that are beyond your understanding, Whitey. Research is one of them, it seems. All afternoon I have been trying to make sure of the exact spot where King Alfred burned the cakes. My head is so tired. I am beginning to wonder if there ever was a King Alfred—and certainly if he ever burned the cakes. I have just come from the library now. My study—the attic upstairs, you know—is just piled to the rafters with the books I brought back with me. And presently I will have to return to my labors, my—er—bibliography. But first I thought you might like to hear a food sermon that I wrote last night."

Chee-Chee's eyebrows went up till they disappeared into his hair, while Polynesia broke out in whispers into her usual and dreadful Swedish swearing.

"Holy cats!" growled Jip. "A food sermon?"

"Yes," said Gub-Gub brightly. "It begins this way:

> "*Dearly Beloved Brethren,*
> *Is it not a sin?*
> *To eat a roast potato*
> *And to throw away the skin?*'

"That is a well-known quotation, first used as a text, I

believe, by His Grace the Archbishop of Batterby. And—"

" 'Ere, 'ere, 'ere! 'Alf a minute," put in Cheapside. "I don't think we quite feel like a sermon this evening, Your Reverence. But what was you digging round after Alfred the Great for?"

"I wanted to put him in my food map."

"And what's the use of a food map?" asked the sparrow.

"Oh, it's a lot of use," said Gub-Gub. " 'The Geography of Food' is a very important chapter in my book. And the food map is an important part of that chapter. I have made several maps and thrown them away because I wasn't satisfied with them. It is so difficult to get the writing small enough to put in all I want. The map should be not only a great help in learning the geography of food but also for the history of food. I would like it to show all the towns where the great events in food history happened—the place, for instance, where Alfred is supposed to have burned the cakes which the old lady had set him to watch while they were cooking. But also the map should mark all the towns and countries that are famous for different kinds of eatables. Such as Melton Mowbray, where the pies come from; the river Neva in Russia—caviar; Yarmouth, famous for its sausages; and Banbury where the well-known cakes are made—that same Banbury, by the way, where we were invited in our childhood to

> *"'Ride a cockhorse*
> *To Banbury Cross*
> *To see a fine Lady*
> *Ride on a white horse.*
> *With rings on her fingers*
> *And bells on her toes.'*
> *Tra-a-la-la, et cetera."*

Gub-Gub finished by waving his two front feet in the air as though he were beating time to music.

"You mean with bells on your trotters and rings in your nose, more like," snapped Dab-Dab. "What a tiresome pig!"

"Still, I don't see what you're going to *do* with this map when you get it finished," said Cheapside.

"Do with it! Why, it will be most valuable," said Gub-Gub. "It tells you where to go to find different things to eat. Supposing you got up in the morning and felt like spending a nice, quiet banana weekend. All right. You just look at the map and take a boat for Central America. Perfectly simple."

"I see what he's getting at, Cheapside," said Jip.

"He's going to have a sort of bill of fare take the place of timetables. All you've got to do is go to a booking office and say, 'I want a ticket to the best pudding you have. First class, please.' Yes, it's simple, all right."

"Tee-hee-hee!" tittered the White Mouse.

"I'm afraid none of you are taking me very seriously," said Gub-Gub. He glanced at the clock. "I'll tell you some more another night. It is the hour for my bibliography. I must go and bibble."

And with great dignity he gathered up his papers and left the room.

THE SECOND EVENING

THE GREAT FOOD AUTHOR SPEAKS OF HIS
RESEARCH INTO HISTORY AND INVENTION
CONCERNED WITH THE ART OF EATING;
AND THE WHITE MOUSE ADDS SOMETHING
FOR THE BOOK

"**N**ow, when we come to take up the history of the discovery of food," said Gub-Gub after the animals were gathered round the fire another night, "we find ourselves faced with a big problem. Many people have written on this subject, but not all of them seriously. Some you might call just food philanderers. And much that is generally believed to be true I found in my—er—research, was not true at all. Take the potato, for instance—a tremendously important article of food. What would we do without it?"

"You'd grow thinner," muttered Jip.

Gub-Gub took no notice of the interruption and went on.

"Take the potato: Its discovery, most people think, was made by Sir Walter Raleigh. Wrong, all wrong. It is true that Sir Walter, in 1586, first introduced it to Ireland, where it is still quite the favorite vegetable—known under the various names of spud, pratie, potatter, etc. But Raleigh wasn't the first to discover it. He only brought it over from the Carolinas and had it grown on his estates—in Cork; and very soon the Cork potatoes spread over the rest of Ireland."

"Tee-hee-hee!" tittered the White Mouse. "Cork potatoes! How splendid! Then they'd float in the stew and you wouldn't have to go fishing for them with a spoon."

"Dear me!" sighed Gub-Gub. "What a lot of things I have to explain to you, Whitey! Cork is a county in Ireland where Sir Walter Raleigh had his estates."

"Well, who did really discover the potato?" I asked.

"An adventurer named John Hawkins," said Gub-Gub. "It was he who first brought potatoes to England in 1563. He found them in common use among the people of South America—at Quito, in Ecuador, to be exact. And that's rather curious too, for in Quito it is almost impossible to boil potatoes."

"Why?" asked Too-Too the owl.

"Because the city of Quito is way up in the Andes Mountains—very, very high. And the water all boils away long before your potatoes are cooked."

"Ah, yes, I've heard of that," murmured Polynesia, who had been a great traveler in her time.

"I don't like potatoes anyway," Jip muttered, turning over on the hearth with a deep sigh.

"Oh, but, Jip," said the White Mouse, "did you ever try them mashed and then baked in the oven with grated cheese over the top?"

"That is called *pommes de terre au gratin*," said Gub-Gub with a superior air. "Then take the parsnip, that queen of all vegetables, known in botany as *pastinaca sativa*. It is found in the wild state on the roadsides in England and throughout Europe and temperate Asia. It has been cultivated since the times of the Romans. Being, as it is, part of the natural order of *umbelliferoe*, it was always—"

"Can't you stick to the English language?" said Jip. "What's all this foreign stuff, the umbrellery-thingamajig and the rest?"

"Oh, don't take any notice of him," snapped Dab-Dab. "He's just trying to make us think he knows some Latin or Greek—and botany too! *Bottomy* would be more to the point, for him—judging from his figure."

"Pardon me," said Gub-Gub politely, turning to the duck. "But no one could think of you as a judge of figures in pigs—in poultry perhaps, but not in pigs. Now, supposing you had ever seen that famous beauty Patricia Portly. I don't suppose you'd have thought hers a good figure."

"Who on earth was Patricia Portly?" Chee-Chee put in.

"She was a very well-bred lady pig," said Gub-Gub. "Came from one of the best families. And ah, there was a figure! Such grace, such curves! She was always spoken of as the Venus of the Berkshires. I must confess"—here the great author smiled a little over memories of bygone days—"that I was quite a bit in love with her myself at one time. I found her friendship most inspiring—for my book, I mean. I had had great difficulty in choosing the best eatables to inspire

Patricia Portly, the Venus of the Berkshires

an author. Someone said that olives were good. But I did not find them so. They upset my temperament."

"What might that be?" asked the White Mouse.

"I'm not quite sure," said Gub-Gub. "But it is something that all authors have. Don't interrupt. Well, to go back to Patricia Portly. She helped me a great deal in trying out the best foods for a writer to work on. Her drawing room was quite famous, and only the most refined pigs were invited to her parties. It was a pleasing sight to see her lolling on a couch surrounded by pigs of importance, pigs whose names were known everywhere, pigs who had really done things. I have quite a piece about her in my book. For she too made a name for herself in the history of food discovery. Yes indeed, she will be known to future students as the inventor of food perfumes. A real pioneer, you might say. At every one of her parties she wore a different perfume: sometimes it was prune juice; sometimes essence of caraway seeds; or nutmeg or barley broth; and she had one that I thought was particularly lovely, a mixture of vanilla and horseradish—very delicate. But perhaps her greatest work of art in this kind of invention was first made public when she got married. She lay awake many nights trying to think up a new scent to be used at her wedding.

You see she wanted a nosegay and — "

"A nosebag, you mean," Jip put in with another grunt.

"She wanted a nosegay," Gub-Gub went on, "which would be something that had never been used by a bride before. And finally she decided on a bunch of Italian forget-me-nots."

"I never heard of the flower," said Too-Too.

"Well, they're not exactly flowers," said Gub-Gub. "They are those long green onions that come in the spring. You see, the very refined pig society in which Patricia moved did not like to call them onions. So they changed the name to Italian forget-me-nots. They became very fashionable after that and were nearly always used at pig weddings. Patricia's wedding was a very grand affair. The only thing that spoiled it, slightly, was that some of the guests, instead of throwing ordinary rice at the happy couple, threw rice puddings. They meant well, thinking that the bride and groom would like cooked rice better than raw. But I must say it *was* a little untidy."

"That porker's imagination," said Dab-Dab. "Well—" She shrugged her wings in despair and said nothing more.

"My chapter on the history of food discovery," said

Gub-Gub, "turned out to be a much longer one than I had expected. Because not only did it have to take in all those naturalists and travelers who had first found new things to eat, but I found that besides the famous Patricia Portly, there were quite a number of others who had invented very clever things connected with eating.

"For instance, there was the man who first thought of, and used, the soup thermometer. He was an Inuit chief. When this gentleman was invited down south to meet the Governor General of Canada, many dinners and parties were given in his honor at Ottawa. And he had to eat lots of dishes that were quite new to him—among them hot soup. And of course he had been used to eating his food cold up in the Arctic Circle—raw seal steak and that sort of thing. Well, he thought the soup was fine, but he burned his mouth very badly on it. And he never seemed to learn the trick of telling when it had cooled down enough. Then one day he saw a thermometer hanging up somewhere. He asked what it was for. And when he heard that it told you how hot or cold the weather was, he said to himself, 'Ah, why not have one for soup.' And he bought himself one—it was really a bath thermometer. And he kept it always on a cord around his neck when he went out to parties and he never burned his mouth anymore and lived happily ever after."

Jip groaned but said nothing.

Gub-Gub turned over some of the papers that lay on the table before him.

"Here's another very clever invention," said he, after glancing down a page of his notes. "The gingersnap hygrometer."

"What's a hygrometer?" asked the White Mouse.

"A hygrometer," said Gub-Gub, taking off his spectacles, "is an instrument for telling you if the air is damp or dry."

"No need for that in England," said Polynesia. "It's always damp. Beastly climate! Now, in dear old Africa it is—oh, well, never mind. Go on, Professor."

"Well, there was a man once who suffered greatly from coughs and colds and asthma and all that sort of thing. And his doctor had told him that he should never go out when the air was damp. Now, you know how gingersnaps get sort of tired and soggy when the weather is damp—they bend instead of breaking with a crack. So this man always kept one on his windowsill and he used to try it every morning. If it bent, he stayed indoors; if it broke, he went out and took a walk."

"But what did he do with all the ones he broke?" asked the White Mouse.

"He ate them," said Gub-Gub. "He had plenty of gingersnaps. He was a baker. But let me tell you about the invention of pebble soup. In Russia, many years ago, when Napoleon was making a nuisance of himself spreading wars all over the place, a very hungry soldier called at a farmhouse to see if he could get something to eat. The farmer's wife, who was alone in the house, had had so many soldiers coming to her door for food that she told him at once she had nothing. She closed the door on him and he sat down outside in the sun and began to think. The soldier felt sure that there were things in the house to eat; but the problem was how to get the farmer's wife to part with them. And suddenly he had an idea. He knocked again at the door. The woman opened it and told him that if he didn't go away, she would set the dogs on him.

" 'Excuse me,' said the soldier, 'but are you interested in cooking?'

" 'Why—er—yes,' said she. 'That is, when I have anything to cook.'

" 'Well, did you ever hear of pebble soup?' asked the soldier.

" 'No,' she said. 'I never did.'

" 'It's very delicious,' he told her. 'I wonder if you would care to have me show you how it is made?'

" 'Yes, I think I would,' said she. 'I'm always interested in new dishes.'

"You see, her curiosity was aroused to find out how on earth anything good to eat could be made out of pebbles. So the soldier put down his pack and gathered up from the yard before the door two large handfuls of pebbles. These he carried into the kitchen and washed the dirt off them with great care. Then he asked for a saucepan, and when he had half filled it with clean water and pebbles, he set it over the kitchen fire. He stirred it from time to time with a spoon. And when it had come to a gentle boil, he tasted it and smacked his lips.

" 'Ah,' said he, 'splendid!'

" 'Let me try it,' said the woman, thinking that some magic had been performed before her eyes.

" 'In just a minute,' said the soldier. 'It needs salt — and pepper.'

"So the farmer's wife went and got salt and pepper and these were added to the soup. He tasted it again.

" 'That's better,' said the soldier. 'But you know, the last time I made this dish — just before we entered

Moscow—I found that a little onion, just a trifle for flavoring, made a great difference. It is too bad you have nothing in the house, as you say.'

" 'Oh, well, wait a moment,' the woman said. 'It is just possible I may find one—one that has been overlooked—in the cellar.'

"She was all interested now to see how this mysterious cooking was going to turn out and she didn't want it spoiled for the sake of a scrap of onion. She brought one and the soldier sliced it up into the saucepan. Presently he tasted the soup again.

" 'What a difference a good carrot would make now,' said he, 'if we only had one!'

"So next a carrot was brought and added to the pot. And once more the soldier tasted.

" 'There's no doubt about it,' said he, 'that I have the touch of the true artist when it comes to cooking. I really should have been a cook instead of a soldier. When this war is over, I may change my trade. Who knows? Much better to feed people well than to kill them!' He took another sip. 'There now,' said he, throwing down the spoon, 'I have done better than I thought. I have no hesitation, good woman, in saying that that is a dish fit to set before a king. But do you know what a really first-class cook would do now?'

" 'No,' said she.

" 'Well, he would add one more flavoring—a bone. The soup is practically perfect as it is. But a really great cook would put in just a bone, or perhaps two— any kind would do, beef bone, veal bone, mutton bone—only for flavoring, you understand, just to give it body, as we say. Well, it is unfortunate that there are no bones in the house. But it can't be helped. Put the plates on the table and I will ladle out the soup.'

" 'The plates are on the sideboard there,' said the woman. 'You can set the table. I've just remembered that I have an old beef bone in the larder. I'll go and get it.'

" 'Oh, in that case,' said the soldier, 'I'll let the pot simmer awhile longer. The pebbles are not quite as tender as they should be yet.'

"So the farmer's wife went and brought a nice beef bone, which was put into the saucepan. And after a little, the soldier ladled out the soup, carefully, from the top, and the two sat down at the table to try it. The woman found it so delicious that she got a loaf of black bread out of the pantry to go with it, and the meal was a great success. It was only some hours later, when she came to wash the dishes, that she discovered the pebbles where they had sunk to the bottom of the saucepan, just as hard and uncooked as they were when they were put in. But by that time the soldier was well on his way to the next town, where there was plenty of food to be had."

"Well," said Chee-Chee, "the farmer's wife wasn't very clever, was she?"

"No," said Gub-Gub. "But the soldier was."

"Where did you get that story?" asked Too-Too.

"From the library—in my research," said Gub-Gub. "But to this day, I understand, it is still told in Russia. And it is supposed to be true too."

"It is too bad," said Dab-Dab, "that you can't find something useful to do with your time."

The White Mouse twirled his long, silky whiskers with both his front paws. There was a thoughtful look in his pink eyes.

"I don't know," said he presently. "It must be rather fun to write a book. I'd like to write one myself. But the only thing I could write would be short stories about cheese, and I suppose they might be tiresome to any readers but mice. Would you like to put me in your book, Gub-Gub?"

"Why?"

"Well," said the White Mouse, "it just occurs to me that I myself have added something to food inventions."

"What did you invent?"

"Well, I wasn't exactly the inventor. I was rather the invention, one might say. I was—er—a pea fielder."

"A *what?*" asked Jip, looking up from the fire with a scowl.

"A pea fielder," the White Mouse repeated in a small voice. "Long ago I told you how, before I came to live with Doctor Dolittle, I was a pet mouse. I was owned by a boy, eight years old. Whenever there were peas for dinner, this boy, although he was very fond of them, had great difficulty in eating them properly. He would try to lift them into his mouth on a knife instead of a spoon. And of course they spilled and ran all over the place. For this he was often scolded by his parents, who hated to have them trodden into the carpets. So the boy used to bring me to the table in his pocket. And he got me to run after the peas when they spilled, catch them, and eat them. And very busy it kept me too. For you have no idea how clever peas are in running away and hiding themselves—under the piano, down rat holes, behind the grandfather clock, everywhere. The boy called it fielding peas; so he ought to be put down as the inventor, although I did the work. I was to get an extra piece of cheese for supper if I left no peas uncaptured. But the boy was an awfully good spiller. And by the time I had caught and eaten them all, I never had any appetite left to eat the cheese. My figure was absolutely ruined. And while the beastly vegetable was in season, I was so round I could roll almost as well as a pea myself. Would you like to put that in your book, Gub-Gub?"

"Oh, yes," said the great author. "I think it's very important. Certainly I'll put it in."

"You would!" snorted Dab-Dab in disgust.

THE THIRD EVENING

THE DOCTOR OF SALAD DRESSINGS, AFTER A FEW
WORDS ABOUT A CERTAIN ANNIVERSARY,
TELLS THE FAMILY CIRCLE THE STORY OF
THE WARS OF THE TOMATOES

The next time that Gub-Gub gave the family an author's reading there was a wintry wind blowing around the house. Chee-Chee, being of African blood, usually found the English weather rather trying, as did Polynesia—only, unlike the parrot, he was not always grumbling about it. Instead, he made himself an excellent wood collector and fire tender. The lively little monkey used to climb the trees in Doctor Dolittle's garden and take down all the dead branches he could find. He also kept the walks and lawns tidy by gathering up the fallen twigs. These he stacked neatly into boxes beside the kitchen fireplace.

Tonight he had a merry blaze roaring for us. But even with this, the room was none too warm for comfort until I had pulled the heavy curtains over the windows and most of us had gathered close around the hearth.

When the great pig author entered the room, we noticed he was wearing the old green coat that had been part of his costume when he had acted in the Puddleby Pantomime. In the buttonhole of this in days gone by he had worn a carnation or geranium to show that he was a smart pig-about-town. But this evening, instead of a flower, the once popular actor was wearing a piece of red silk ribbon.

"What's the decoration for, Perfesser?" asked Cheapside.

"That," said Gub-Gub, seating himself at the table, "is for the anniversary."

"Let's see," said the sparrow. "Today's the third of September—no, don't tell me—well, I give up. What anniversary is it?"

"Today is the anniversary of Yorkshire pudding," said Gub-Gub.

"You should have known better than to ask him, Cheapside," Jip growled.

"Decorations are always worn on great anniversaries," said Gub-Gub, looking over his spectacles toward the dog. "All people who are really well-educated eaters wear a red ribbon to celebrate that day when, many years ago, that great institution, Yorkshire pudding, was invented and placed upon a British dining table for the first time. It is a very important date in history. What did you ask me for if you are only going to be flippant and silly? After all, I do my best to enlighten your ignorance."

"Our *pignorance*, you mean," said Jip. "Nobody likes a good meal better than myself. But how on earth you manage to write and talk so much about food is more than I can understand."

With the manner of a patient, weary schoolmaster, the great author took off his spectacles and laid them beside his papers on the table.

"Now, what is the use," he asked, "of anyone pretending that eating is not important?"

"The Perfesser is quite right there," said Cheapside. "A bloke can't get far without grub. Wasn't it Napoleon what said, 'An army marches on its stummick'?"

"Maybe that's why camels can go so far," said Chee-Chee. "They are supposed to have two stomachs, aren't they? Or is it some other animal?"

"Tee-hee-hee!" tittered the White Mouse. "Two tummies! What a wonderful idea! Still," he added, growing suddenly serious, "maybe it wouldn't be so good—always. Fancy having two stomachaches at the same time. Oh, my!"

"But don't forget, my friend," said Gub-Gub, "that if you got one stomach out of order, so long as you had two, you could always use the second one to carry on with. But can't you see,"—he turned and waggled his enormous quill pen at Jip drowsing on the hearth—"that the story of food discovery is the history of the human race—the history, in fact, of the whole animal kingdom? Ask Doctor Dolittle himself—and even geography. How do you suppose the different races of people came to settle down where they are on the map today? Because they could get what they wanted to eat there. Or because they got pushed there by other people who wanted the same things to eat."

Gub-Gub got up and waved his pen still more wildly at his listeners.

"Many of the greatest wars in history, ladies and

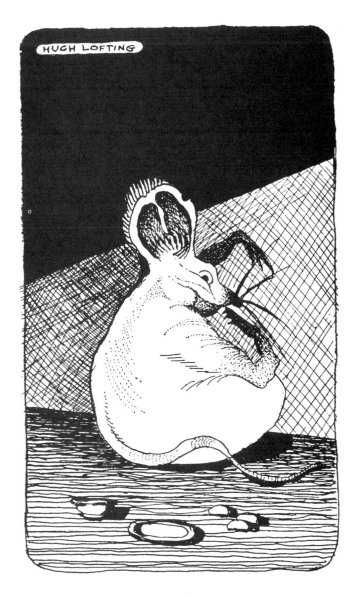

"Tee-hee-hee!" tittered the White Mouse

gentlemen, have been fought over nothing more than wheat to make bread with, or oatmeal to make porridge out of, or lands where the best grass grew to feed sheep and goats on. The sheep's wool was used to make clothes to keep people warm and the goats' milk was used to keep them from starving. But they couldn't get along without having first the grass. Food! And drinking water—another form of food, after all: Tribes have fought tribes for hundreds of years over who should own wells and rivers that meant life itself to them. Whole nations have disappeared from the face of the earth because of famine—nothing to eat. Great kingdoms have tottered and fallen because the larder was empty. Mighty empires have risen to power and glory—on full stomachs. This book I am writing will show that there is nothing, ladies and gentlemen—absolutely nothing in this world—of greater importance to all of us than food."

The pig author sank heavily into his chair, seemingly weighed down with the earnestness of his long speech and the terrible importance of food.

"Did he say something about goats' milk?" murmured Jip sleepily. "Horrid stuff! Never could stand it."

"Your ideas ain't 'alf bad, Gubby—for the most

part," chirped the cheerful Cheapside. "Nobody's denying that it's grub what makes the world go round. But what Jip 'ere meant was: Why be talkin' about it all the time?"

"Well, why not?" asked Gub-Gub. "It's nothing to be ashamed of, is it?"

"Oh, no," said the sparrow. "Go on with yer lecture, Doctor Hog."

"Please don't call me 'hog,'" said Gub-Gub peevishly. "I wish you would remember that I have a pedigree—a long pedigree."

"A short tail and a long pedigree! Tee-hee-hee!" whispered the White Mouse, tittering over his own joke.

"Well," Jip grunted, "I'd rather have a short pedigree as a fox terrier than a long one as a pig."

"There you show your ignorance some more," said Gub-Gub. "There have been knights of old who were proud to bear upon their shields and crests the sign of a boar's head."

"What is a boar?" asked the White Mouse.

"A pig who talks too much," growled Jip.

"Don't mind 'im, Perfesser," said Cheapside. "'E 'as to 'ave 'is little joke, yer know."

"Well, now," said the great author, "you have

heard of the Wars of the Roses—where one side wore the white rose of Lancaster and the other the red rose of York when they went into battle?"

"It was a little before my time," said Polynesia, who had led a very long life. "But I do remember hearing about them."

"Very good," said Gub-Gub. "But did you ever hear about the Wars of the Tomatoes? No? Well, I'll tell you about them."

The White Mouse polished his long, silky whiskers again and settled down to listen. "The Wars of the Tomatoes! That ought to be good," he giggled.

"In a certain country," Gub-Gub began, "many years ago, the regular dish for Christmas dinner was roast goose stuffed with tomatoes. For as long as anyone could remember, this had been a national custom. People would no more have thought of going without roast goose with tomato dressing on Christmas Day than they would of flying. Fine, round red tomatoes were grown on the sunny hillsides of that fair and peaceful land specially for stuffing the Christmas goose, and all would have gone well with the happy simple folk if, one evil day, a certain gardener had not come to visit them from a neighboring country.

"The gardener was not himself a bad man, and

although his coming caused no end of trouble, he meant well. He considered himself a great expert in growing new sorts of vegetables and fruits, and he brought with him a new kind of tomato. It was a yellow tomato—that color when it was ripe, I mean. And he told the people it was the latest and most fashionable thing—that nobody who was really up-to-date would dream of using the old red tomatoes if he could get yellow ones. Well, you know how folks are: They always think that anything that comes from a long way off, from a foreign land, must be better than that which is made or grown at home.

"So many of the richer families started to grow yellow tomatoes, and very soon the new fad spread and was taken up quite widely. And when the next Christmas came around, many a roast goose was stuffed with yellow tomatoes instead of red ones. But in every land there are always people who are called conservatives— that is, those who believe in keeping to the old ways of doing things. And the conservatives in that country began to get annoyed when they found that the Christmas geese were being stuffed with something new. They made speeches in the marketplaces. They called on all good citizens to take a firm stand against yellow tomatoes. Red ones, they said, had always been good enough for their fathers and should be good enough for them and for their children. It was a nasty foreign custom, they felt, creeping into their homes from enemy nations beyond the border, and if yellow tomato dressing was allowed to spread farther, their beloved native land would never be the same again— the country would just go to the dogs."

"The dogs would not have taken such a silly country as a gift," sniffed Jip. "We don't care for tomatoes anyway."

Gub-Gub raised his quill pen for silence and went on.

"On the other hand, the wealthy people—not the older families, but those who had just become rich and wanted to make a name for themselves as fashionable and up-to-date—they stuck to the idea of the new goose dressing. Soon they too began getting up at street corners and making speeches to the people. No end of a fuss was raised. The whole country was divided. Arguments and rows went on all over the place. The government was upset. Ministers lost their jobs. All sorts of unexpected things began happening over this question that looked as though it would never be settled. At last real war broke out, the worst kind, civil war—a people fighting among themselves."

"Were there many killed?" squeaked the White Mouse in a hushed voice.

"No," said Gub-Gub. "Fortunately not. It is perhaps the only case of its kind in history. For the Wars of the Tomatoes were indeed peculiar. Although they lasted a terribly long time, spreading over many Christmases—so that people began to wonder if they were ever going to stop—not a single person was killed. That was because they used tomatoes instead of bullets and cannonballs. One side called themselves the Yellow Party and the other the Red Party.

"But perhaps the most peculiar thing about the whole struggle was that the Red Party threw yellow tomatoes, and the Yellow Party threw red tomatoes. You see, they thought it would be more insulting to bombard the enemy with his own stuffing, so to speak."

"Well, who won?" Chee-Chee asked.

"Oh, the Yellow won," said Gub-Gub. "They at last managed to corner the Reds in a steep valley between two high hills. And there, on the bank of a stream, they simply smothered the enemy under a perfect mountain of tomatoes till they begged for mercy and peace was declared. But it is said that long after the war was over the river ran red with tomato juice."

"So the yellow tomatoes were used for stuffing after all, eh?" asked the White Mouse.

"Oh, no," said Gub-Gub. "You see, there wasn't a tomato left in the country after the fighting stopped. They had all been used up in those terrible battles. Next Christmas, in fact forever after, the roast goose was stuffed with onions."

"Humph!" said Cheapside. "A very juicy bit of 'istory, Perfesser—still, if you must 'ave wars, I reckon that's as good a kind as any. From what I can make out, there ain't been none of 'em what's brought much more profit to either side than that—just a valley full of ketchup. Heigh-ho!"

"Ah, but the loss in vegetable life," sighed Gub-Gub, shaking his head sadly. "All those tomatoes! A race wiped out. Terrible, terrible!"

"Never mind," said Chee-Chee, putting another log on the fire. "Just think what a good thing it was that the people weren't arguing about coconuts."

THE FOURTH EVENING

AFTER EXPLAINING THE VARIOUS THINGS
THAT HIS ENCYCLOPAEDIA CONTAINS,
GUB-GUB BEGINS HIS FAMOUS
"FOOD MYSTERY STORY"

"Before you begin again, Perfesser," said Cheapside, "suppose you give us a general idea of the layout. I mean, what else 'ave you got in this bloomin' encyclo-pediddy of yours besides 'istory and geography?"

"Oh, lots and lots," said the author. "There are chapters on food poems; food music; food fables and nursery rhymes—'The Fox and the Sour Grapes,' 'Plumpudding Hot, Plumpudding Cold,' 'Miss Muffet and the Curds and Whey,' the Real Story of 'Little

Jack Horner,' never before printed, etc. And food romances—that's quite a big section. It gives you, among other things, the love stories of famous cooks and the food life of famous heroes. Then there's a chapter on food fantasy, but I must warn you it's rather highbrow stuff—needs lots of imagination, you know, and—er—soul to understand it properly —pure food fantasy, very whimsical. So is the part on food fairy tales. Oh, and there's lots more: food detective stories, cooking crimes, and kitchen mysteries, etc.; food comedies; food tragedies. I have even started a food Shakespeare."

"Lord save us!" gasped Dab-Dab. "Of all the impudence, of all the outrageous cheek I ever heard in my born days, that takes the cake. A food Shakespeare! What are you going to do—write the man's plays over again for him?"

"Er—well, not exactly that," said Gub-Gub. "But, you see, I thought it might encourage the education of young people—and of young pigs even more so. Very little has been done to make learning of any kind attractive to young pigs. Even now that John Dolittle has invented a Piggish alphabet, they don't do much serious reading. The works of William Shakespeare—or Shakespoon, as I call him in my encyclopaedia—are very important to a good education. And I felt that by putting a little more about food into his plays—just changing words here and there—I might give young pigs a taste for good books."

"I knew a goat once who ate books," said Cheapside. "But 'is taste wasn't very good. 'E liked the cheap magazines best. Read us some of your new Shakespeare, Gubby."

"Well, I haven't gotten very far with it yet," said Gub-Gub. "I'll just give you a few quotations from it, and then you can see the sort of thing I'm trying to do."

He turned over a page or two of his notes.

"Ah, here we are," said he presently. "This is from the tragedy of *Macbeth*: 'Lay on, Plumduff! And burst be he who first can't hold enough!' You see the alteration is very slight. And here's another. This is from that beautiful and romantic play *Roly Poly and Juliet*: 'Oh, Roly-o, my Poly-o, Wherefore art thou, Roly-Poly-o? A dumpling-o by any other name would smell as sweet.' Isn't that nice?"

"A bit doughy and oh-y," muttered Cheapside. "But I get your idea. Now, 'ow about these food detective stories you was speaking of?"

"Yes, let's have another food story," said the White Mouse. "I liked that one about the pebble soup. Maybe you have one about a piece of cheese?"

"Not among the detective stories," said Gub-Gub. "Those are what is called a series, that is, they have many of the same characters, the same people, in all of them. The chief character is a man called Sherbet Scones, the famous 'icebox detective.' He runs through the whole collection of mystery stories."

"Well," snapped Dab-Dab, "I hope he keeps on running and doesn't stop. I don't want to meet him."

"This detective was very clever," Gub-Gub went on. "Whenever things were stolen and the police were unable to find out who did it, Sherbet Scones was nearly always called in to catch the thief. It was the case of the missing eggs that first made his name known. That was when a certain very important Indian rajah was traveling around Europe to see the different countries. He had with him, besides his son, a great number of servants and a terrible lot of baggage. His favorite dish was curried eggs, and he had brought along with him three cases of eggs. Ordinarily a case of eggs is not very expensive. But these were awfully valuable. They were a special kind of sea bird's eggs that could be found only on the shores of this rajah's own native state—and even there they were nearly priceless.

"Sometime after he got to England the first two cases were all used up. And one day when the rajah had invited a lot of people to lunch, and was going to treat them to his famous curried eggs, the cook came running to him in a frantic state, crying out that the third, and last, case of eggs had been stolen. There was a great commotion. Not only was the rajah dreadfully upset over having to disappoint all these guests in his house—most of whom were looking forward to his famous curried eggs—but the police, as soon as they heard about the business, were extremely angry. What would the world think of England now, they said, when important visitors had their very lunches snatched from them? Well, two rewards, both of them large sums of money, were offered. One was offered by the rajah to anyone who would get back the stolen eggs, and the other was offered by the police to anyone who could find the robbers and bring them to justice.

"Well, this cunning Detective Scones found out who it was. And you'd never guess. The rajah had been stopping at the university town where he planned to have his son go to college. Now, this university had a secret eating society, or fraternity, called Sigma Eta Apple Pie—after the Greek letters, you know. They used to hold secret meetings once a month, very gay affairs, at which each member in turn had to supply some entirely new dish that had never been eaten by the society before.

"Sigma Eta Apple Pie was formed, I understand, because many people felt that the British, usually so brave and adventurous, were very unadventurous in eating. And it's true, we are, you know—no doubt about that—always eating the same things, very few dishes, when you think of France and other countries—no eating courage at all. And one of these lighthearted college boys, when it came around to his turn to think up something new to eat, had been very puzzled where to find it. Then he had heard about the visiting rajah and he thought curried sea birds' eggs would be just the thing. So he broke into the house and stole the rajah's last case of eggs. The young man had a very rich father, and he had meant to get the money to pay the rajah for the eggs afterward. But when he found that the eggs were worth almost a fortune, and that the police were after him, he decided to hide—both himself and the eggs. The great Sherbet Scones tracked him down and found him."

"Where?" asked the White Mouse.

"In the secret icebox of the secret society," said Gub-Gub. "It was marvelous because no one knew where it was, nor even that it existed, except the members of the society. But Scones got only one of the rewards, the one offered by the police."

"Why, who got the other one?" asked the White Mouse.

"Nobody got the rajah's prize for the return of the eggs because the young man had eaten them. And he was nearly frozen too when they took him out of the icebox. So that was how Scones first came to be known as the 'icebox detective.' And after that he was called in on a great number of robberies, particularly those connected with food in any way; he was spoken of as a specialist in that kind of work. Police departments of other cities came to him for advice and help, and food robbers in every corner of the earth trembled at his name.

"But what I really started to tell you about was the hardest detective job that Sherbet Scones ever did. For the day came when the great detective found himself working against a mastermind—brains, daring, brilliant brains almost equal to his own. A whole string of robberies had suddenly broken out, like the measles,

Scones, the "icebox detective" — in disguise

you might say. Nobody seemed able to find out who had done them, or how they were done. No clue was left behind which — "

"No glue was left behind, did you say?" asked the White Mouse.

"No *clue*," repeated Gub-Gub patiently. "That is, no trace or other thing that would give anybody an idea who the thief might be. Please don't interrupt. No footprints could ever be found around the houses robbed; no fingerprints ever gave the clever thief away. After several of the robberies had been written about in the newspapers, people set guards around their houses, who stayed up all night with loaded shotguns. They put special bars and locks on their doors and windows. They rigged up all kinds of tricky alarms — wires strung across the floors so they rang bells if anyone should sneak in and trip over them in the dark. And still, all the time, houses were broken into and things were stolen."

"What sort of things?" asked the White Mouse.

"Wait. I'm coming to that," said Gub-Gub. "Night after night Scones the detective lay awake in bed gnashing his teeth in despair — when he wasn't gnashing them through the silent streets, trying to find out who it was who so outrageously defied the law. You see, as I told you, he had built up a great name for himself. And as the weeks went by and no one was caught, he felt that his reputation was at stake—that he would no longer be considered a great detective, the greatest specialist of his kind in the world, unless he caught somebody soon and put an end to the chain of robberies.

"And then too, the newspapers were so mean to him. They kept saying what fools all the police and detectives were and how poorly they protected honest people against evildoers. One newspaper—it was a food newspaper called *The Daily Meal* with offices in Grub Street—was particularly mean to poor Scones. As the robberies were all connected with food, *The Daily Meal* was very interested in them, and it told one of its men to give all his time to them.

"This man's name was Hamilton Sandwich. He was called Ham Sandwich for short, and just Ham by those who knew him very well. He was considered by his paper to be its very best and smartest reporter, for he was simply marvelous at getting food news ahead of anybody else. Well, Ham Sandwich followed Scones around wherever he went and made a great nuisance of himself pestering the detective with questions, trying to learn what he had found out. And when Scones wouldn't tell him anything, he went back to his office and wrote sourcastic remarks for his newspaper to print about the stupidity of detectives in general and of Sherbet Scones in particular.

"But the 'icebox detective' had not been idle — not by any means. By carefully examining all the houses broken into, be began to put certain things together in his mind. For instance, he noted that the thief, or thieves, always got in by the pantry window. That was at the beginning of the robberies. Later, when most pantry windows were protected with special locks, they got in some other way — often without leaving any trace at all as to how they had done it. Most mysterious! But Scones noticed also that no matter by what way the robbers got in, they always *visited* the pantry and apparently they always ate a light meal there before they went away. Because every time there were dirty plates and knives left lying around, showing that food had been eaten. And also *there was always one plate left on the floor of the pantry.*

"On discovering these things, Scones set to work to find what kinds of food seemed to be the thieves' favorites. And he found that whenever the pantry contained strawberry jam, a pot or two had always been opened. 'Ah-hah!' he snarled. 'A thief with a taste for strawberry jam, eh? This must be investigated.' And he hurried off on the scent with the tireless Ham Sandwich close at his heels.

"He went to police headquarters and started looking through the records. Now, these records, as they are called, are drawers and drawers full of cards that are kept by police departments, showing a history of every thief who is known from past robberies. But though Scones spent a whole day hunting through thousands of cards, he could find none that told him anything of a thief who always helped himself to strawberry jam when robbing a house. He was puzzled, baffled. But presently he had a thought. 'Ah-hah!' he said again. 'No record here? Must be a foreigner, then. A foreign criminal with a taste for strawberry jam. No matter, he shall never escape the icebox detective!' And he hurried away again, tiptoeing past Ham Sandwich, who had fallen asleep among the records.

"Then he sent messages all over the world to the police of other cities, asking if they knew anything of a daring thief who was fond of strawberry jam. But though he got many answers, none of them gave him any information of such a person. Scones was baffled again. Meanwhile new robberies almost every night were committed right under his nose, you might say. And he went on gnashing his teeth—while Hamilton Sandwich went on writing nasty things about him in *The Daily Meal.*

"Now, about the kind of things that were stolen: at first the great detective noticed that all sorts of different plunder were carried away—though never very much at a time—clocks, silver spoons, a little jewelry, suits of clothes, walking sticks, telescopes, cigars, etc. This also made it hard to tell who the thief might be or what kind he was. But one thing the police nearly always do when they are puzzled in this way is to watch the shops kept by receivers of stolen goods."

"What are they?" the White Mouse asked.

"Receivers of stolen goods are men who buy things that have been stolen. They are careful not to ask where the things have come from because they know, or guess, that they have usually been taken from other people's homes. They pay a very low price for the goods and sell them for a much higher price. It is a regular trade but a dangerous one and certainly not honest. I had a pig friend once who was a well-known receiver of stolen vegetables. He was looked down upon by the best people in pig society as a very shady character. But it must be said for him that he never sold the plunder over again. He—"

"He ate it all up," Jip put in. "I'll bet a ham bone on that."

"Exactly," the great author agreed.

"That's what you call 'playing safe,'" Polynesia remarked. "Clever rascal."

THE FIFTH EVENING

THE FOOD MYSTERY STORY IS CONTINUED—AND ENDED

"Well, to go on with my story," said Gub-Gub, "by keeping an eye on the receivers of stolen goods, the police are often able to run down an umbrella or a banjo or a hot water bottle or some other thing that has been stolen. Everywhere he went, Sherbet Scones carried with him a list of missing articles taken in the robberies. But he could never find a trace of a single one of them at the receivers'. He set some of his assistant detectives, disguised as chimney sweeps and tax collectors and whatnot, to call at their shops every so often and nose around. But nothing came of it. Nevertheless this time, instead of being baffled, he learned something—or, rather, deduced something."

"De-juiced something?" asked the White Mouse mildly. "You mean with a lemon squeezer?"

"Oh, dear, dear, dear!" cried Gub-Gub. "*No!* De*duced*. That's a word used a lot in the best mystery stories. It means using your brain, if you've got one. Reasoning. You notice some small thing and you chew it over in your head for a while and presently it leads you to a new idea. For instance, suppose you came into the room here with your whiskers all gummed up with treacle. I would look at you a moment and then start thinking, and finally I would deduce that you had been to the larder. Is that clear?"

"Well," said the White Mouse timidly, "maybe. But it seems to me that you would have deduced that I was just as untidy an eater as yourself. Which I'm not. But never mind. Go on."

"Now, Sherbet Scones deduced this way: He said to himself, 'If the thief is not taking the things to the receivers, what *is* he doing with them? He must be shipping them out of the country so his friends can sell them for him abroad. Ah-hah! Another link in the chain. No record with the police here. Friends abroad helping him. Why, he *must* be a foreigner—a nasty foreigner. Yet why have I not heard something about him from the police of other countries? A criminal as clever and experienced as this one must have a record somewhere. Strange! Strange!' He felt another attack of being baffled coming on and, hoping to shake it off, he went home to write a letter to his grandmother with rheumatism.

"The dawn was just coming up in the east when he let himself in with a skeleton key. The cat came out as he opened the door and began to drink the morning milk on the doorstep. But Scones didn't care. His mood was reckless and disgruntled.

"He went straight to his study and flung himself into a chair. On his desk he noticed a pile of letters, the morning mail that had just come in. Glum and brooding, his thoughts far away, he began idly turning over the letters. He came to one with a foreign stamp on it. Savagely he tore it open with his teeth. He hated everything foreign that morning.

"But as he read the letter his mood changed. His eyes popped. His mouth dropped open. The scowl on his features turned slowly into a wide grin. For the letter was from the chief of police in Venezuela, in South America. You see, Scones had forgotten to count all the answers he had gotten to his own letter, and this one, from a country such a long way off, had taken many weeks to reach him. It said:

" 'We feel almost certain that the man you are after is one whom we have had on our records here for three years past. He usually enters houses by the pantry window. Always stops to eat strawberry jam on his way out — that is, if he can get it. But any jam will do. In fact, seems fond of all kinds of food. Not a native of this country, but well known here as Chillibillibeano, the Texas Pantry Bandit. Chilly for short. Does he use a dog to help him? If so, you can be sure it's Chilly.'

"Sherbet Scones sprang up from his chair. He sprang so suddenly and so high that he banged his head on the ceiling. But he was so excited he never even noticed it.

" 'A dog!' he shouted. 'Why, of course! The plate on the floor. What else could it be for but a dog?'

"At this moment one of his assistants rushed in to say that another house had been robbed just down the street. The great detective quickly disguised himself in a long white beard and hurried away to examine the scene of the crime. As soon as he got to the house he questioned everybody in it. But, as usual, no one had seen the robber getting in or getting out, and, as usual, there were signs of a meal left in the pantry —

jammy knives and spoons — *with one dirty plate left on the floor*. Scones then searched around outside the building for tracks of a dog. And, sure enough, he found them in the kitchen garden under the pantry window. So he was now quite sure that Chillibillibeano was the gentleman he was after. And the first thing he did was to put a piece in all the newspapers:

"WANTED FOR ROBBERY

Chillibillibeano, known as the Texas Pantry Bandit. Tall, dark, and thin. Slippery customer. Fond of jam. Works with dog. Anyone knowing anything that may lead to the capture of this desperate character will please write to, or call upon, Mr. Sherbet Scones, detective.

"And now everybody knew the thief's name and what he looked like, and there was a great deal of talking and guessing everywhere. But just knowing a robber's name and a few things about his looks doesn't mean you've caught him. In bygone days Robin Hood and Captain Kidd were well known and famous many years without being captured. And now in spite of all the chatter and gossip and everything, no one came forward who could say he had ever really seen this mysterious man whose long list of thievings had caused such a stir.

"And presently Scones began to wonder and doubt. Could it be Chilly after all? Surely a stranger would be suspected when everyone in the neighborhood was looking for him. Houses were broken into just the same as before, almost every night. But now the things stolen were always food. No jewelry or umbrellas anymore—just food. And such quantities! Careful housewives who had laid in large stores when things were cheap would have their whole supply carried off—sacks of flour, barrels of apples, a dozen jars of chutney in one night—which puzzled the great detective mightily. Because this was more than any one man could eat or want for his own use. It almost looked as if some gang—and not a single robber—were at work.

"So Scones said to himself: 'Very well, then. Suppose we *are* mistaken. And if we can't find the man, let's see if we can find the dog.' And he went back over the dog tracks and examined them all carefully through a magnifying glass. Then he made sketches of them. These he took to the dog breeders and dealers. They said they had never seen paw prints like them before and had no idea of what kind of dog it could be. Which was not surprising, because, just as Chilly was a brand-new kind of robber, so the dog he was using as a helper was a brand-new kind of hound."

"What was the breed called?" I asked.

Gub-Gub smiled to himself in a superior sort of way.

"It was a Sneakinese," he said.

"A what?" yelped Jip, starting up.

"A Sneakinese," the author repeated. "It was a cross between a Pekinese and a sneak—a sneak thief, you might say. Very rare. You see, for robbing pantry shelves and iceboxes in the dead of night it is terribly important not to make any noise. A clumsy hand reaching in to get a jar of pickles or a can of salmon can cause enough clatter to rouse the Seven Sleepers. Now, the Sneakinese had a very sharp, thin nose and a long, wormlike body. He could thread his way between bottles of vinegar and tins of tea and fetch out a bunch of asparagus without so much as a tinkle. He had been specially trained; and he never ate the things he was sent after because he knew that when his work was done, his master would prepare a nice midnight supper for him on the pantry floor before they made their escape.

"All this came out afterward. The dog remained unknown, unrecognized, and uncaptured up to the last, because, like Chilly himself, he wore a number of different disguises. Sometimes he was dressed up like a cocker spaniel; sometimes like a dachshund. And he always acted the character to go with the particular disguise he was wearing. Some days he would hobble about town dressed as a thoughtful Scotch terrier, very old, puffy, grizzled, and feeble. Other days he'd be a friendly Airedale puppy, frisking all over the place and talking to everyone. He could bark and growl in six different tones of voice. He could look crosseyed if necessary. He could do everything. And of course no one got wise to him since he was never the same. There is no doubt about it that both Chillibillibeano and his dog had brains, great brains.

"The Texas Pantry Bandit, after his description appeared in the papers, became more daring and cheeky then ever. It almost looked as though he didn't care what he did. He took a mischievous delight in leaving notes behind him, at the houses he stole from, deliberately signed with his own name: 'Thanks for the nice supper. Your guards are too stupid for words. Anyone could get through them. Yours truly, Chilly.'

"He loved to tease Scones by calling him a flatfoot and a fathead. And he would actually tell him in these notes which houses he was going to rob next. And even when the 'icebox detective' went to the houses and stayed up all night with two assistants and a dozen policemen, the best and most expensive food was found mysteriously missing the next morning.

"Then the police rounded up all the dogs in the town, every one, and had them claimed by their owners. And out of sheer devilment the Sneakinese came too. But he came dressed as a stray cat—half Persian and half starved—frightened, soft-footed, and mean. And the disguise was so perfect, no one knew him from the real thing; and after getting a good square meal free, he spat at the other dogs and took his leave.

"Meanwhile, folks were getting more and more annoyed and indignant that the thieves were not caught. And Sherbet Scones went on gnashing his teeth. He had gnashed them so much that they were nearly all worn away, and he was very miserable because he couldn't eat properly. The papers went on making fun of him, and Ham Sandwich brought out a comic poem on the front page of *The Daily Meal*—at least Ham thought it was comic:

> "*When the night falls, deep and stilly,*
> *Through the pantry window Chilly*
> *Grabs great joints of beef and bones.*
> *What's the use of Sherbet Scones?*'

"At last, however, Chillibillibeano went too far.

He had stolen the most precious kinds of foods; he had made a laughingstock of the best detectives; he had thrown defiance in the teeth of the police; he had puzzled the world with his daring brilliant villainy. But now he did something he had never done before, something that, perhaps, no one had ever done before: He stole a cook."

"What on earth for?" asked Chee-Chee.

"Why, cooks are very valuable," said Gub-Gub. "That is, good ones. And this one was marvelously good. She was famous for her pastry—for her rhubarb pie in particular. Her name was Vanilla Verbena. Her mistress used to say that she was worth her weight in gold—and in her case that meant a good deal because she was as big as a house and weighed a ton. Now, a strange thing began happening at the house where Vanilla Verbena worked. It had been broken into and the pantry robbed several times. The family was a large one to cook for: mother and father and six children, all with hearty appetites.

"Ordinarily they had been a very plump, well-fed-looking lot. But suddenly they started to get thin—especially the cook herself. That good woman's figure, which had been as round as an apple, shrank and shrank till it got positively scrawny. People said that maybe it was because her pantry had been robbed so often and that the worry over losing all that beautiful pastry as soon as it was cooked was making her thin.

"But be that as it may, suddenly she disappeared. Her bed, which had specially strong springs to carry her weight, was found empty one morning. Sherbet Scones at once got busy, busier than he had ever been before in his busy life. The seriousness of Chilly's new crime was not the only cause. Scones had a private reason—a romantic one—as well.

"You see, while he had been working on the robberies at this house before, the 'icebox detective' had met Vanilla Verbena when she was still plump and comely, and after tasting her wonderful pastry he had decided it would be a good idea to marry her. He had even had the kitchen in his own home made larger so there would be ample room for her to work in. You can therefore imagine his rage, his furious indignation at Chillibillibeano, who had now added to his long list of evil deeds the unpardonable one of cook snatching. And he swore by his worldwide reputation, by his long false beard, that he would neither rest nor close his eyes till his precious Verbena was found and the wicked foreigner was thrown into prison.

"She was as big as a house"

"Well, he nearly died for want of sleep, but he did it.

"And this was how: First he did a lot of deducing. He asked himself, why should a man steal a cook? Because he liked good food? Of course. But after the robber got her, he couldn't put her to work in any house of his own because she was known by sight and would be recognized. He must be planning to use her to run a restaurant for him. And of course it would be a new restaurant, one just opened within a short time.

"So Scones set out and traveled all around, asking everyone about new eating places. And he went to all these restaurants and ordered rhubarb pie. He knew, of course, that Chilly would keep Verbena out of sight. But Scones remembered the taste of her famous rhubarb pie, and he was certain he could tell it from all others.

"In his travels he ate so many helpings of pie that he often felt he could never look another one in the face. But he kept bravely on. And sure enough, at last he came to a restaurant where the waiter served him rhubarb pie that he at once knew could be no other than Vanilla Verbena's very own. At once he had the owner of the restaurant arrested and handcuffed by one of his assistants. It was Chilly himself beyond any doubt.

Then Scones made a thorough search of the place, and in the kitchen he found his darling cook chained to the pastry board still making rhubarb pies — also there was a strange-looking dog eating out of a plate on the floor. And that was the end of the wicked career of the Texas Pantry Bandit."

"Did he get sent to prison for a long time?" asked the White Mouse.

"No, that is the odd part of it: He never went to prison at all," said Gub-Gub. "While Scones was taking him to the police station in a cab, he began questioning the robber about several matters. For one thing, he wanted to know what Chilly had done with all the food he had stolen. And he found that the Texas Pantry Bandit was really a sort of Robin Hood in disguise. He had been robbing the rich to pay the poor. Whenever he found out that one wealthy family had large stores of food and kept a particularly good table, he would make a point of breaking into that house and feeding the poor people, who hadn't enough to eat, with the food he stole. Even Vanilla Verbena, the famous cook, he had carried off for the sake of the poor. He wanted to have a restaurant where tramps and hungry people who had no money could come and get good meals for nothing.

"But he was indeed a clever rogue. Seeing that Verbena was too big to push through the pantry window — or, in fact, to carry off by any man at all — he got a lot of reducing pills, medicine for thinning people down, and every time he broke into that house he put some into all the food in the larder. And that was how the whole family as well as the cook had lost so much weight.

"Now, when the 'icebox detective' heard why his great enemy had done all these robberies, a great change came over him. He could not bear to think that a man who had been so noble as to spend all his life in the service of the poor should be sent to prison. On the other hand, he at least had to make it look as though he meant to bring him to justice and punishment. So after thinking silently for a while, as the cab rolled along, he said to his prisoner:

"'You would no doubt like to have a smoke. I will take off your handcuffs so you can get your cigars out of your pocket.' This he did, and Chilly thanked him. Then he said, 'Supposing you were a free man now instead of on your way to jail, would you lead an honest life or would you go on robbing houses?'

"And Chilly said, 'I would lead an honest life. At this robbing game one is bound to get caught sooner or later. Besides, I owe it to the Sneakinese. He was a perfectly honest dog when I first got him—from the circus where he learned to be so clever at disguises. But it was I who led him astray and taught him to steal.' He sighed sadly. 'If I were a free man now, I would take the Sneakinese and go on the stage. I can play the guitar very well. Alas, that it is too late for me to turn over a new leaf!'

"Again Scones became strangely silent, chewing on his false mustache, wrapped in thought. Suddenly he said, 'Excuse me a moment, I want to get out and speak to the cab driver.'

"He knocked on the window, stopped the cab, and got out. He was careful to leave the door open behind him. Pretending to give some orders to the driver, he watched Chilly out of the corner of his eye. And he noticed the Texas Pantry Bandit sneak away into the bushes, followed by his faithful dog. But Scones made no attempt to run after him.

"He got back into the empty cab and drove to the police station. There he asked for the officer in charge and said, 'I'm very sorry. I caught the thief and had him all handcuffed and everything, but he escaped from my clutches while I was bring-ing him to the jail. However, I feel sure you will be bothered with no more food robberies.'

"Then he went off and married Vanilla Verbena. And she got her beautiful plump figure back and they both lived happily ever after."

THE SIXTH EVENING

HOW QUINCE BLOSSOM
SAVED HER FATHER'S LIFE

"This is a food fable," said Gub-Gub. "It's from the Persian."

"What is a fable?" asked the White Mouse.

"Gracious me!" said the great author. "Sometimes I think I ought to change your name to Mr. Whatsit! Every time you open your mouth you begin with, 'What's a this?' 'What's a that?' A fable is an old story that is sometimes meant to teach a lesson but is not necessarily strictly true. A fellow called Aesop wrote fables. Aesop was, I believe, a cousin to Milksop, but of that I'm not sure. Anyhow, he was a member of the well-known family of Sops—all writers, poor fellows.

"Well, in the days before Persia was formed into a regular country, there was a very warlike people that lived in those parts, called the Bashibaloukas. They were great horsemen. They lived in the saddle, you might say. In spite of being a very wild tribe that terrorized the whole of the Eastern world, they were also a very clean lot—most particular about taking regular baths. It was, in fact, a religion with them. Daily washing was commanded by their prophets and high priests. But they didn't have to worry about it, like going to church. Their horses took care of it for them. Living in the saddle, as they did, they also slept there. And the horses were so well trained that as soon as daybreak came they made straight for the nearest water. So, if you were a Bashibalouka, you usually woke up before breakfast, swimming in a river full of ice, or treading water at the bottom of some nice deep pond. This made the people very hardy.

"Well, the Shah of the Bashibaloukas decided to go to war with his most powerful neighbor, the Sultan of Kinkidoo. He got all his army washed and fed and set out for battle. For several months neither side won or lost much, because the Shah could not seem to draw

his enemies into a good businesslike fight. The soldiers of Kinkidoo kept to the mountains, where they
could not easily be followed. And one day the Shah
called his commander-in-chief, General Pushpoud-
ul-Pish, into his tent and said, 'General, in mountain
fighting the Sultan is too clever for me. I can't get near
him. I have therefore decided what I must do.'

"'Yes, sir?' said the General. 'What is your plan?'

"Now, I should have told you at the beginning that
this is a fable about poisons—a poisonous tale, you
might call it!"

"Poisons!" said the White Mouse in a very shocked
voice. "I don't think I like that. What has poison got
to do with food?"

"Oh, a great deal," said Gub-Gub. "There is a long
chapter in my book on poisons. A knowledge of food
teaches you what is good to eat, while a knowledge of
poisons teaches you what is good *not* to eat. Both are
important. You have all most likely heard that old
saying, 'One man's meat is another man's poison.'
Ostriches can eat things that would kill you and me—
tennis balls, pebbles, and whatnot. But all poisons are
not deadly. Some just give you a pain or make you sick
for a while. In ancient times, when people studied
poisons a good deal more than they do now, you could

buy all sorts: a half-hour stomachache, a two-days-in-bed pill, or a few drops of innocent-looking tonic that could kill you dead in five minutes.

"Well, in those wild times, long, long ago, all kings and queens and people who were really important kept regular poisoners in their pay, and they lived in the palace along with the rest of the household. They were something like the royal doctors of today — scientists, regular chemists, you know. Anyhow, to go back to where I was: the General of the Bashibaloukas said to the Shah, 'What then, O Mighty Monarch, is your plan?''

"And the Shah answered, 'General, since I cannot draw the Sultan into open battle, I think it would be a good idea to poison him off. Once the army of Kinkidoo is left without this very smart leader, my men, I feel sure, can knock it silly in no time. Go you therefore and bring me all the Royal Poisoners, in order that we can have a comfortable chat and decide the best means to dose the Sultan in such a fashion that he will never again lead his troops in war.'

"At these words the General turned deathly pale. And I'll tell you why in just a minute.

"'Great Shah!' he cried, falling on his knees before his master. 'We brought no poisons with us. The day before your army marched away from the capital, they had a grand feast. It was sort of a club dinner to which all the professional poisoners were invited. And somebody thought it would be a good joke to give them a little of their own medicine. Anyhow, something was put in the soup, and all the poisoners were so sick the next day they couldn't travel with the army!'

"The Shah frowned a terrible frown. 'What, no poisoners!' he cried. 'I never heard of such a thing!' And he started stamping up and down the royal tent like a crazy man.

"Now, the reason that the General had turned so pale was not at the thought of poisoning off the Sultan of Kinkidoo. To the hardy cavalrymen of the blood-thirsty Bashibaloukas that was a mere trifle. But besides being commander-in-chief, Pushpoud-ul-Pish was also the Shah's Grand Vizier. And in those days if you were a Shah or an Emperor, and anything went wrong, the first thing you did was to chop off the head of your Grand Vizier, throw him away, and get another one—for anything at all. If the horses went lame, or the hens stopped laying, the Grand Vizier paid the penalty with his life. That's how you showed you were an important leader and not to be trifled with.

"The poor General started to sneak out of the tent, but as he left, the Shah shook his fist at him and cried, 'Before the sun goes down you shall pay for this with your head!'

"Miserably Pushpoud-ul-Pish made his way to his own tent. There he found his wife and his beautiful daughter, Quince Blossom, both fast asleep. He woke his wife and told her the sad news. 'Alas!' he cried, wringing his hands. 'This is the end of me!'

"But the General's wife was a very bright woman. In fact, some people said she was a much better general than Pushpoud-ul-Pish himself. Instead of getting excited, she went into a long think. She was looking at this beautiful daughter, Quince Blossom, sleeping peacefully on her couch of Bokhara embroidery.

"'Listen, Push,' she said presently, 'it is a poor head you have, but it is the only one you possess and we can't afford to lose it. Even in this great army, husbands are scarce. Yonder maiden may yet save your life. Right well you know, for all her beauty and her innocence, she is the worst cook in the world. Ever since she nearly killed His Majesty's sacred elephant when she prepared his rice for him, has she not been forbidden, by royal command, even to boil water lest she burn it and injure the hardy manhood of our army? Very well, then: the Shah's poisoners have been left behind. I propose to use our little Quince Blossom instead. If we can only smuggle her into the Sultan's camp, to be employed as cook for him, I'll warrant he will die of indigestion before the setting of the sun.'

"Then very gently she woke up the beautiful damsel and explained the plan. She told her daughter that their family could not well afford to lose its head, and it was clearly the girl's duty to save her father, even if the work were by no means to her taste. Now, Quince Blossom was born what you would call a homebody — domestic and housewifey. The thing she most desired in life was to raise a pious family and cook good meals for a good husband. So Fate had been very unkind in making her the most terrible cook that every swung a saucepan. And when she learned what it was her mother wanted her to do, she broke down in sobs and her tears ran all over the Bokhara embroidery of the couch.

"Nevertheless, for her father's sake, in the end she gave in and said she would go. The best of the Bash-ibalouka scouts was summoned at once. And in a large fruit basket, covered over with pineapples for sale, she was carried up through the mountains and smuggled into the Sultan's camp. There the famous scout left the basket in the marketplace while he went around and did some scouting and spying.

"He found out that, luckily, the Sultan was in need of a new cook. Good! Also he learned that the Sultan that same day had planned to poison the Shah. Poisoning was altogether too fashionable about that time. The scout could not afford to waste any time because he had to introduce the new cook as soon as possible and then hurry back to the Shah to warn him of the plot against his life.

"But he was a good scout and knew his business. He hustled back to the marketplace, got Quince Blossom out from under the pineapples, and took her before the Sultan. He boasted that she was the finest cook in the world and was especially good at pancakes. The Sultan said he would try her and see what her cooking was like. The girl was put in the royal kitchen and the scout hurried away.

"Well, she killed her man all right. After the first pancake the Sultan was carried to his bed and never left it again alive. Two of the best generals in the enemy army too died from the same meal. Poor Quince Blossom! She thought she could never forgive herself. She knew she wasn't a good cook. But she hadn't really tried to make the pancakes specially bad. They just turned out that way. For her, bad cooking came naturally. It was a kind of a gift, you might say. Nor could anyone feel very sorry for the Sultan, since he had himself planned to poison off his enemy also. Nevertheless, Quince Blossom, as soon as she knew her dish had turned out successfully, wept all over the kitchen and ran away back to her own people.

"There she found the Shah's court holding a big holiday and everybody was very happy and gay. Her father, the Grand Vizier, was given presents and honors by his delighted master. The Shah himself sent for Quince Blossom to thank her, and he told her she had won the war for him. Because, with the death of the Sultan, the army of Kinkidoo was already in full flight before the swift and hardy cavalry of the Bashibaloukas. He offered her the post of Chief Poisoner to the Royal Household. But she refused, again bursting into tears at the thought of what her pancakes had done.

"The Shah took the maiden on his knee to console her. And then he noticed, when she removed her veil to wipe her eyes, what a very beautiful girl she was. The Shah was a bachelor himself and he promptly asked her to be his queen instead of his poisoner. She said she would be glad to if he would promise that her father's head would never be chopped off whether the hens laid or not.

"This promise he gave her—he even said she could do all the cooking she liked too—so long as he and his army never had to eat it. He said it had better be buried, so the horses and dogs couldn't get at it.

"And so they were married amid great rejoicings and they both lived happily ever after."

THE SEVENTH EVENING

THE PIG AUTHOR, AFTER A FEW WORDS ABOUT
DIET, TELLS HOW A BEAUTIFUL SUNSET ONCE
INSPIRED HIM TO WRITING SOMETHING
TRULY HIS OWN

Again there was a fine fire roaring up the Dolittle
kitchen chimney—to keep away the chill of the year's
early days which so often lead us into believing that
summer has begun when winter hasn't really gone.

The good Chee-Chee was dragging broken boughs
across the floor, and those too heavy for him to carry he
rolled before him like a barrel. Much dust and bark
were left behind on the way, but the monkey looked
after that with the hearth broom. And when he took

his seat to listen, the kitchen floor was clean and spotless enough to satisfy even Dab-Dab herself.

John Dolittle was fiddling with an aquarium up in his study—where he was trying to make rare water plants take kindly to indoor life. The housekeeper never permitted anyone—on any account—to interrupt his work.

Everybody else was gathered in the kitchen. We had now come to make a pleasant habit of listening to Gub-Gub's readings. Dab-Dab still treated his writings and discussions with the contempt she felt they deserved. But we noticed that she nearly always came to listen, and we had begun to suspect that she thought the encyclopaedia of food not quite as rubbishy as she had at first declared. Besides that, she no longer shooed us off to bed at the regular hour. So that sometimes the pale blue of the morning sky was glimmering at the windows before Gub-Gub had done talking to us about the art of eating.

Too-Too the owl and Polynesia the parrot never said a great deal about anything at any time. And for this reason they perhaps earned a reputation for being very wise without much work. I myself was always interested, because I never knew what surprise the great pig author would spring on us next.

Cheapside, the London sparrow, and the White Mouse enjoyed quite openly Professor Gub-Gub's lectures, roaring with laughter or giggling like schoolchildren when some particularly crazy passage took their fancy.

Even the grouchy Jip interrupted less and less, and when he did, it seemed as though he was rather pretending to criticize—because he thought it was perhaps his duty—than giving his real opinions.

The Doctor of Salad Dressings was this evening somewhat late in appearing. And when he at last showed up, the White Mouse, who had for half an hour been twirling his sleek white whiskers impatiently round his pink nose, demanded the reason for his lateness.

"Well, for one thing," said Gub-Gub, "I've been reading over *The Book of Food Dreams*."

"What's that for?" asked the White Mouse.

"Oh, it's not a very important work," said Gub-Gub. "Rather trashy. But I thought I would look into it just the same. It pretends to tell you the meaning of dreams about food. For instance, if you dream you are eating broccoli, it says you can be sure that some calamity or accident will happen to you. On the other hand, if you should dream you have had a hearty meal of turnips, you are likely to be successful — very soon — in business or love.

"But the thing that delayed me most this evening was my visit to Doctor Pillcrank. Doctor Pillcrank had been advertising in the papers that he could reduce people's weight by mental treatment instead of by dieting."

"What is dieting?" asked the White Mouse.

"Dieting," said Gub-Gub, "is doing without all the things you like to eat and eating all the things you *don't* like. I had been getting rather stout, and I thought I would try this mental treatment, which sounded so much better than the usual one of dieting. But I was very disappointed. The main part of Doctor Pillcrank's treatment is to make you say to yourself over and over again the same thing: 'Tummy, tummy, go away and don't come back another day.' It seemed to have no effect upon my figure whatever.

"Provided you said this to yourself several times a day, he let you eat anything you wanted *mentally* — that is, in your mind. He wrote out for me beautiful meals — artichokes, potatoes, spaghetti, stuffed dates, Welsh rarebit, etc. — which I was told to *think of* at breakfast, lunch, and supper. And that was supposed to give me all the nourishment I needed. But it didn't. It merely gave me a terrible appetite. And all I was allowed to take was a little barley water at morning and noon. The rest of the time I was just to think about eating. And if I hadn't had the presence of mind to put three or four apples under my pillow at night, there is no knowing what would have happened to me. I don't think I'll go back to him anymore. He charged a lot of money and called it Dr. Pillcrank's Mental Treatment for Obesity."

"Obesity?" asked the White Mouse. "Is that the same as obeastliness?"

"Yes," growled Jip.

"Before you came in," said the White Mouse, "we were having a little discussion about your book. I was taking your part. I said I liked the food stories best. But Chee-Chee said that he expected a good deal of the book was just made up out of your head. Jip said he didn't believe anyone could make anything out of your head—except perhaps packing cases. But Chee-Chee was sure he was right, because most of your stories ended, 'They all lived happily ever after.' And that's the way that fairy stories usually end, isn't it? We would like very much to know how much of the book you really did make up."

Gub-Gub cleaned his glasses carefully. He was

silent a moment. And we were all sure that a very important announcement was coming from the Doctor of Salad Dressings.

"What you say brings me to a special part of my book," he began, "which I have purposely kept till the end—that is, till the end of my readings. You see, I felt that beside the bibliography, the library searchings into food history, geography, legend, and so forth, I would like to do a little something that would be entirely my own. I have done it—and I am very proud of it."

"Is it a food story?" asked the White Mouse.

"In a way, yes, it is," said the author. "It should perhaps be called a 'food novel.' And yet that isn't quite the word either. I didn't know what to call it, so I invented a word for it myself. It is an *epicnic*."

"And what may that be?" growled Jip.

"An epic," said Gub-Gub, "is a poem—a poem of importance, or a history tale in poetic language. The story of Helen of Troy, by Homer, for instance, is an epic. But this work of mine, to make it more foodish, more appetizing, you might say—I called an epicnic: the word *epic*, scrambled with *picnic*. It is the story of King Guzzle the Second, or the 'Picnic King.'

"The way I came to begin it was peculiar. Most people have an idea that we think only of food. This is not strictly true. When you see a row of young pigs with a wistful look upon their fresh faces, you must not always suppose that they are daydreaming merely of potatoes. Well, one lovely afternoon I was myself gazing out over a beautiful summer landscape, bathed in the crimson light of an August sunset. I was chewing thoughtfully on a horseradish root, but my mind was full of poetry — chockful.

" 'After all,' said I to myself, 'I am a country pig — a country gentleman. That city life is all very well for a short spell — for a change, you might say. But when everything's said and done, there is nothing like the country. Consider this lovely scene before me: rolling, grassy hills; lush meadows fringing the mere.' You see, that's where the poetic part comes in: to say just 'lush meadows' wouldn't mean much, but 'fringing the mere' at once draws a living picture for us. A 'mere' is a sort of lake; 'lush' means green, well-watered, and grassy — but not squdgy or muddy — splendid hunting ground for sweet lily roots and the like.

"Well, to go on: 'shady copses; the cool, slow river wandering and wiggling down the broad valley; plump, nutty-tasting acorns, lying in bushels beneath the spreading oaks, with little mushrooms popping up like buttons in between; gorse clumps with friendly rabbits running in and out; tall clover in full bloom waving to the gentle breeze; ripe blackberries hiding coyly in the hedges; crab apples crabbing around all over the place.' A scene to delight the heart of any poet—a scene, in fact, of which someone said, 'Where every prospect pleases and only Man is—'

" 'But hold!' said I to myself. 'Do I smell truffles? By my trotters, indeed I do! But I will not dig for them. I will not be tempted. Earthy thoughts shall not interrupt my mood sublime.' You see, I was getting more and more poetic as I went on. I leaned back among the cowslips on the grassy bank and half closed my eyes. Quite possibly I might have starved to death from sheer poetry. Such a thing has happened—to truly great writers—before today.

"But a bee came and stung me on the nose. I suppose he smelled the clover I had been eating. But such was my feeling of friendliness to all Nature, I did not even allow this to interfere with the gentle spirit of my thoughts. And besides, my snout is tough, and not even an angry black hornet can affect it greatly when I am filled with verse and fantasy. I merely raised a cool dock leaf and laid it on my face. Presently I ate it— even poets have to have some nourishment.

" 'Yonder pleasant prospect,' said I, 'needs only a

little of my masterly imagination to make of it the opening scene to a great play, a food opera, a poem of good taste—what you will—something that shall be read and recited by good eaters for all time to come. Here is the first act laid out before me. For is not this the "Picnic Kingdom" itself?'

"I leapt to my feet, burning with the fire of inspiration. Two more bees stung me as I got up—for it appeared I had been sitting on a nest of them. But I took no notice. Grasping my notebook, I set to work. I wrote and wrote and wrote. After I had finished the notebook I began on dock leaves. When there were no more dock leaves, I wrote on anything that came to hand. I even ran after a cow who was browsing near and made notes all over her. I was full of ideas.

"And as I worked, the story of King Guzzle the Second came to life before me in that beautiful scenery that might have been made for him. Darkness fell without my noticing it. And with the daybreak a farmer's boy arrived to milk the cow. I tried to make notes on him too, for I was now roused to a perfect frenzy of inspiration. But he wouldn't let me. So I did my last lines on the trunk of a tree instead.

"When the sun rose in all its glory, I stopped at last—tired, worn out, thirsty, and hungry, but happy—happy as only an author can be who knows he has done his work and done it well. I fell fast asleep—while the cow ate up all my dock leaves and rubbed the notes off herself by rolling in the grass.

"But it didn't matter. The great epicnic was safe in my mind. I went home and wrote it out on wrapping papers. And I will now, with your permission, read it to you."

There was much rustling and shifting of chairs. Chee-Chee rolled a large log on the fire. And the White Mouse gave his whiskers an extra twirl before settling down to listen.

THE EIGHTH EVENING

THE LIFE STORY OF GUZZLE THE SECOND,
KNOWN AS THE "PICNIC KING." OF THE STRANGE
COURT HE HELD; THE CURIOUS MANNER OF HIS
LIFE; OF HIS TREMENDOUS WEALTH. HERE THE
AUTHOR BEGINS THE EPICNIC (WHICH HE HOPES
WILL LIVE AS LONG AS SHAKESPEARE). HE
DESCRIBES THE GREATEST OF THE KING'S FAMOUS
PICNICS AND THE PECULIAR GUESTS WHO WERE
INVITED TO IT FROM ALL PARTS OF THE WORLD.
HE SPEAKS OF THE KING'S FRIENDSHIP FOR THE
GREAT CHRISTOPHE PLANTIN. AND OF HOW THE
FRENCHMAN'S SONNET CAME TO BE ENGRAVED
ON THE GOLDEN SAUCEPAN WITH WHICH
GUZZLE HIMSELF COOKED ON HIS BIRTHDAY

"Now, the Guzzles, even before they were kings,
had always been a family of noble high degree, second

to none in the land. The old man, spending his days in fighting, had been widely known, and feared, as a most powerful prince. Later, when he was crowned as Guzzle the First, he made his country very rich by adding to it conquered lands. Long after he passed away his skill and cunning in warfare were spoken of and remembered. His reign was looked back upon by high and low alike as the Age of Chivalry, when knights were bold, ladies were fair, and soldiers were proud to be numbered in his army.

"Therefore when his son, Guzzle the Second, came to the throne, there was much talk about what manner of king he would turn out to be. With his respected father's memory to follow as an example, it was quite clear from the outset that he'd have to be a great man indeed to come up to the expectations of the people.

"Most folks thought he would start his reign off with a nice big war, so as to make a good impression with a lot of victories that would add still more lands to the Realm of Guzzledom.

"But they were greatly surprised to find that he did nothing of the kind. Instead of calling up his knights in armor and having war trumpets blown all over the place, he sent for his Lord Treasurer and hundreds of clerks who could tell him how much money he had in the banks and what the condition of the Royal Treasury was. He knew that his father had left the country well off, but even Guzzle the Second was astonished when the bankbooks were looked into and examined. He found that he had become king of the richest realm in all history. Old Guzzle the First had been very economical, and never let a cook buy a new apron without a special order from the Lord Treasurer, signed with the Royal Seal.

"'Why, then,' said the new King to himself, 'have any more wars, when the Royal Treasury already has more money than it can spend?' Buying gunpowder to blow off, and new armor to get cracked, seemed simply silly in the circumstances. Instead, he at once gave orders that all the cooks should have new aprons, and caps as well; that all the royal gardeners should have new suits of clothes; that new dishes of gold and silver be bought for the Royal Dining Hall; that new sties be built for all the pigs; new stalls for all the cows, with milk pails of solid pewter, etc., etc.

"You see, he had decided that it was no use trying to earn a reputation as a soldier to match his father's, and that he would therefore make a new kind of reputation for himself. His father had been known as 'Guzzle the Warrior'; he meant to be famous in history as 'Guzzle the Spender.'

"And oh, how he did spend! At first the Lord Treasurer and the Chancellor of the Exchequer would come running to him five or six times a day with bills a yard long, saying that he must be careful, that this kind of thing couldn't go on. The country would be ruined, they said, rich as it was. But Guzzle the Second would just wave them aside and order a set of new silver horseshoes for his favorite horse.

"And after a while—as things turned out—they began to see that perhaps he was right. To be a king or queen in the eyes of the world, you had to have money in those days, the same as you do today. It cost an awful lot to run a country that was at all important. And very soon folks the world over decided that Guzzle's kingdom must be the richest of all because it spent the most. Traders came from every corner of the earth, anxious to open shops and to do business. And instead of getting poorer, the Kingdom of Guzzledom seemed to grow richer and richer the more it spent.

"Now, King Guzzle took to eating in a serious way. Not that this was anything new, of course. Kings must eat, the same as farmers. And many great princes have become famous for the wonderful dishes that they invented. Cardinals and grand dukes have not thought it beneath them to go into the kitchen and attend personally to the preparation of meals that carried their fame to all corners of the civilized world.

"But King Guzzle the Second was greater than all these. After he had made the country prosperous and famous everywhere by his wild extravagances of every sort — so that it became a saying common abroad to speak of a man as being 'as rich as Guzzle' — he settled down to the serious matter of good food in a way that surprised the world. And the world was beginning by now to be surprised fully and often by that monarch.

"Eating was never raised to a higher art. Fortunes were given to a scullery maid who thought of a new sauce. The chef, that is the head of the cooks, became so important a personage in the Royal Household that ministers from foreign lands usually went to the kitchen first, to have a chat over the pots and pans, before making their official bows in the Royal Chamber of Audience.

"And then the dinners and luncheons that he gave! He would be second to none, he said, in the magnificence of his dining room. But he liked best of all to eat *al fresco.*"

"Al *who?*" asked Cheapside.

"*Al fresco,*" said Gub-Gub. "That means, 'out of doors,' in — er — Italian."

"Oh, just something furrin," said the sparrow. "I

thought for the moment you was referrin' to my old friend Al Freshface. Great old bloke was Al! Always saved the crumbs of 'is bread and cheese for me. 'E was a cab driver. Go on, Perfesser. I didn't mean to hinterrupt."

"Well, it was from this pleasant habit of feeding outdoors that Guzzle the Second came to be known to future generations as the 'Picnic King.' He had many other titles of great distinction: Grand Master of the Order of the Golden Fleas, Knight of the Garter and Suspenders, etc. But throughout his long and busy life he would always rather hear his subjects speak of him as the 'picnic king' than under any other name.

"He formed what was known as the League of Rations — a sort of international club devoted to good food. It became famous in history.

"But the picnic that King Guzzle considered his greatest work of art, and that will probably be remembered for all time, was given in the month of July, when the much-loved king had passed that time of life called middle age. Nothing of its kind had ever happened before. Guests were invited from every corner of the earth.

"The Grand Picnic took place in that lovely spot I have already described to you. The Great Sward was thronged with chefs, footmen, and serving maids waiting on the guests, who are said to have numbered not less than a thousand persons.

"It would be absurd for me to try to give you here every name from a list so long. However, the complete Roll of Honor was written down in a special book in the library of the Royal College of Cooking. Many foreign names appear, because the royalty and nobility of other lands were most eager to do King Guzzle any compliments they could, since he was so rich and his money such a power in the world.

"Very well, to begin with, there was the Queen of Blenheim-Orange with her daughter, Princess Mignonette of Marjoram and Rue; there was Prince Pudge, heir apparent to the throne of Greece and Gravy—his father was very desirous he should attend the Grand Picnic. And it must be said that Prince Pudge certainly did his father's kingdom great credit: He ate so much, his war horse was quite unable to carry him home, and special arrangements for a coach drawn by six span of oxen had to be made.

"Vladimir, chief of the Don Cossacks—you can imagine how a man from such a distant territory would be thought highly important—even if he did throw a ham bone at another guest he didn't like.

Such would be a small matter in Vladimir's own country—but created a mild sensation at the polite court of King Guzzle.

"Many other kings and queens flocked from east and south and west and north, and when, on account of family matters at home or affairs of state, they were prevented from attending in person, they sent important ambassadors in their place. For example—Belini Anchovy, Dictator of the Republic of Rhubarb, had a revolution on his hands; but his uncle, Don Castro Castor Oil, came in his stead. Good-looking he was— very, but not at all popular. The Duke de Barleduke, always bothered by the gout, was represented by Ambassador Linseed. And so on.

"But by far the greater part of the guests were made up of the landed gentry; those who, while of noble blood, were famous for their country pursuits rather than for being descended from this royal line, that Grand Duchy, or from the other reigning house. Men of the land they were; and it was with them a matter of greater pride that the whole world knew the excellence of their cattle, the quality of their asparagus, or the honey raised by their bees than all the knightly deeds in Morte d'Arthur or the families of the Domesday Book. And it was for this reason—because they were, so to speak, specialists beyond compare in their particular line—that they had been invited to the Grand Picnic of Guzzle the Second.

"To mention a few: There were Sir Lancelot Lollipop, famous rescuer of Distressed Damsons. The Dutch naturalist Viscount van Veal, whose work on vegetable botany had caused such a stir. Conrad, Earl of the Marshmallows. Gumbo Goulash, of Budapest, whose Danube dairies supplied the finest butter in the world. Sir Cinnamon Bunn. The two Scottish lairds of high renown, both heads of their clans, Sir Benjamin Butterscotch and Sir Haggis McTavish. Lady Viola Vinaigrette, who raised the finest melons in the country. Madame O. Gratin, the best-known hostess in Paris.

"Sir Simeon Sausagely was there too—he who was supposed to know more about the raising and training of water spaniels that any man living. Her Grace, the Duchess of Doughnut, specialist in French pastry— specialist in eating it, that is. Sir Marmaduke Marmalade, direct descendant of the House of Orange. Fatima, the Sultana of Chutney. The Countess of Curd, who had given her whole life to cream cheese. Young Nubbin, the Brussels Sprout, of noble lineage. Judge Juniper, who was later to marry Lady Dredful

Manners—a very gay young person—and there was much talk about the difference in their ages. The Dowager Countess of Caramel Custard. And that highly important person in the eating line, the Marchioness of Cling and Cloy.

"The King himself had lately given more and more of his time to the farm, the country, fish and game preserve, etc. The business of state, which he had found very tiresome, he was content to leave to his ministers—and notably to his nephew, of whom we shall have more to say later.

"The ladies were indeed well represented. Some folks said that it was because they were fonder of food than men—which started a terrible argument—while others claimed it was because they had less business to attend to and were naturally keen about picnics and parties.

"Be that as it may, certainly a terrible lot of them came, and they seemed to enjoy themselves heartily. Among them was that charming little débutante Sticky Fudge—equally good at lace making and riding horses. She had only just been presented at Court, so her mother came along with her.

"Another girl who was very popular with the young men at the food dances was Pepita Pancake from

Madrid. She had a regular chaperon. Played well on the harp too, did Pepita Pancake, simple things; but after all she was only a flapper, you might say.

"Last, but by no means least, there was Squire Squab of Squelchley-on-the-Squeam, renowned for the raising of pigeons. So worldwidely important was his fame in this respect that the King considered it a compliment that he honored the Grand Picnic with his presence.

"It was generally feared that the beloved King might eat more than was good for his health, and some other monarch be elected to take his place. However, for the present, Guzzle the Second seemed sound and hearty, and he liked nothing better than to go into the kitchen to try his royal hand at cooking. He was indeed quite good at it. He would put on a silken apron and, with the Chief Cook acting as assistant, he would prepare special dainties in the Golden Saucepan.

"The Golden Saucepan had a history to it and became an institution of wide fame and importance. The King remained a bachelor all his life; otherwise it would have been presented on the fiftieth anniversary of his wedding. But instead, when his fiftieth birthday came and went, and he was still unwed, his loving subjects all subscribed what small sums of money they could afford and gave him a saucepan of peculiar design, wrought of solid and pure gold.

"Now, as it happened, the King's birthday was also the day when that great dish, steak and kidney pudding, was invented. This the Court took to be a happy sign of Fortune and good luck. Just as some people are born under the sign of the lion and Venus, so it could be said that King Guzzle the Second was born—in a manner of speaking—under steak and kidney pudding. And that is how His Majesty's birthday, which was celebrated throughout the land with great rejoicing and ceremony, came to be known not only as 'King's Day' but also as 'Steak-and-Kidney-Pudding Day.'

"So important did the King consider this odd happening in connection with the date of his birth, that he issued a Royal Decree that so long as he lived he would act as cook in his palace kitchen on that day, serving his people with the famous dish prepared as it had never been prepared before.

"Thus, year after year, when his birthday came round, the King's henchmen, high and low—foresters, falconers, gardeners, gamekeepers, and whatnot—foregathered in the lofty dining hall and made merry while the greatest monarch of his time served them steak and kidney pudding with his own royal hands from the Golden Saucepan. They held high wassail—"

"What's wassail?" asked the White Mouse.

"I'm not quite sure," said Gub-Gub. "But it is something you always held at great feasts in ancient times."

"Oh," said the White Mouse. "A napkin very likely."

"About this time there was in France a great printer and poet of the name of Christophe Plantin. The King much admired this man, and had him specially invited to the palace. Among his works is a sonnet called 'The Happiness of This World.'

"King Guzzle the Second, at fifty, had given up many of the wild extravagances of his early days, and he meant to spend the remainder of his reign in teaching his people how to live—not just eating and drinking, but the true art of living, sauced with good sense and a knowledge of things real and worthwhile.

"Christophe Plantin seemed just the man to help in this, and the King, when presented with the Golden Saucepan, summoned the Court Engraver and bade him chisel on the sides of that noble vessel, just as it was written, that poem 'The Happiness of This World.' Of course it was in French—and Old French at that. So I will not bother you with foreign wording."

"No. You'd better not," growled Jip.

"In translating it into English I have been most careful to stick to the sense," said Gub-Gub, "almost word for word. All I have done is to change the position of a line or two here and there."

The great pig author cleared his throat and started his recitation. And though the White Mouse tittered at the beginning over the idea of a mere pig turning French into English, he and the rest of them were oddly solemn when the poem ended.

THE HAPPINESS OF THIS WORLD

Sonnet

TO HAVE

A comfortable house, beauteous and clean;
 A garden where the well-pruned, scented
  branches lean;
Some fruits; some vintage rare;
 A little group of children; servants few;
Cherishing, without boast, the faith
 Of helpful housewife fair.

To have no debts, nor pride,
    Nor quarrels, nor fussings with the law;
Nor business disagreements with relations over
        money.
    Satisfied with little,
Expecting nothing of the Great,
    All planning built in faith upon a model fair.

Reposefully awaited in this house of mine,
    The knowledge of the value of these things,
Shall make the Coming of Life's End,
    Instead of something dark and grim
The pleasant Visit of a Gracious Friend.

THE NINTH EVENING

THE TRUFFLE TROUBADOURS, THE RIVER OF
LEMONADE, THE JAMMING CONTEST, AND OTHER
THINGS BRIGHTENING THE GRAND PICNIC,
WHICH LASTED MANY DAYS

"Many are the tales told of the King's wild junketings. But most of them I am much inclined to doubt—especially after the coming to the Court of that great naturalist, poet, and philosopher, Christophe Plantin. No man ever lived with more sense and peaceful beauty.

"But I ought, however, to give you some idea of a few of those peculiarities of King Guzzle that set tongues to spinning strange yarns in odd corners of the earth.

"For instance, it was he who invented the Alarm Clock Menu. On retiring at night he never gave such orders as, 'Wake me at six o'clock' or 'Let me sleep till nine.' He would say, 'Wake me with fried eels' or 'I would be aroused tomorrow's morn with griddled wheat cakes, garnished with chervil—be careful not to omit the chervil.'

"Now, ordinarily it would be supposed that these were the dishes he meant to eat for breakfast. Not necessarily, at all. In the morning he was quite likely to send the food down to the royal kennels, or make a present of it to one of the cottagers. All His Majesty had wanted was the *smell* of the cooking to wake him up by.

"He didn't care to have fussy valets come and tell him what hour it was. Hours meant very little to His Majesty, whereas smells did. The fragrance of a perfect kitchen—that was different. You could lie in bed an extra twenty minutes or so, pondering over whether you really felt like fried eels; or making up your mind if griddled wheat cakes with chervil garnishing were truly worth getting up for. He had a long list of dishes for this purpose, and before he said good night to his company, the First Lord of the Bedchamber always came to him and said, 'Shall the Lord

Chamberlain arouse Your Majesty with grilled kid-
neys tomorrow, or mushrooms on toast?' "

"Why, I never heard of anything so stupid!" said
Dab-Dab. "What a scandalous waste!"

"Not at all," said Gub-Gub. "I've already told you
that the food was always given to the dogs or the peas-
ants. Besides, it is so much pleasanter a way of being
waked up than having someone tugging at the bed-
clothes, yanking up the blinds, and gabbling about
how late it is."

"But," said the White Mouse, "I don't see how you
could be sure that just a smell of cooking could wake
you up."

"Ah," said Gub-Gub, "that shows that you are not
what is called a real genius in the art of eating. Once I
took a furnished apartment to live in — well, it wasn't
exactly an apartment — they were too expensive. I
hired a clothes closet with a hot water pipe running
through it. Quite comfortable and much less expensive. And the woman across the hall used to wake me
up every morning at six o'clock by cooking hot gingerbread. Regularly to the minute. I never — never in
my life — could sleep through hot gingerbread. I suffered agonies of insomnia. It was no use. I had to leave
and go to live somewhere else.

"Well, another thing that must be put down to the credit of King Guzzle the Second is the institution of the Truffle Troubadours. In those days, you must understand, all great courts had troubadours. Sometimes they were just wandering minstrels who picked up a little money here and there by singing a song at a feast. And yet other times they were regularly attached to the household of a king as court musicians, poets, and songsters. Their special job was to make up long lays, as they were called—historical poems that would last through eight or nine courses—usually about the warlike deeds of the king or other great person who kept the troubadours in bread and butter.

"Guzzle the Second had not much use for war or deeds of military glory. And though he was probably the richest man in the world, he was, by and large, a very modest man and withal a gentle soul. He therefore thought it would be a good idea to have his troubadours, instead of spouting long lays about the bravery of his ancestors in battle, sing songs of food and compose poems about things to eat. He hoped in this way to give good appetites to his guests. Nothing upset him so much as to have a perfect dinner prepared and then to find that no one was hungry enough to eat it. By good kitchen music he often made languishing ladies quite peckish and the heartiest of his huntsmen ready to eat the battlements off the castle walls.

"Again I must restrain myself, for the songs and poems and roast-beef roundelays he ordered composed were many. One piece that was very popular began:

" 'The Tripe-and-Onion Troubadours
Came traipsing through the gate;
For Lady Popsy Peppermint
Was dancing very late.'

"It had twenty-five stanzas. Another was a very touching little thing about the jealousies of Apple Charlotte and Brown Betty. Then there was a rollicking song concerning the Legend of the Milksop and the Hard-boiled Egg. Another: 'Gather Ye Radishes While Ye May' was always being called for. The Chief of the Troubadours was often sent for to recite a series of delicacies in verse that gained great favor with the ladies—when they were busy at their tapestry before luncheon—called 'The Salad Sonnets.'

"But enough of that. The palace of King Guzzle the Second was peculiar in more ways than one. The Royal Artists, instead of decorating the halls with portraits of kingly ancestors in full dress, painted the walls with what is called *still life*—that is, pictures of fruit and cold salmon on platters, onions and peaches in full bloom, and the like. And I must say it added greatly to the brightness of the Royal Dwelling. Castles are too often made unnecessarily gloomy with pictures of sour-faced dowagers with curses and pimples, and cross-eyed princes on horseback in full armor. Above all things, the King liked to make life cheerful for his fellow men; and no one could blame him for putting peach trees in full bloom and boiled salmon surrounded by lifelike cucumbers in place of sour-faced dowagers and gloomy, cross-eyed princes.

"And then, architecturally speaking, the palace was quite out of the ordinary too. Usually in the castles of kings the various parts of the building are given such names as the Bloody Tower, Traitor Hall, the Haunted Chamber, and such like. Noble families are proud of these names—though why, no one has ever been able to find out.

"King Guzzle changed all this. He gave orders that no matter what a particular part of the castle had been known as in his father's day, cheerier names would be used in future. That is how folks came to speak of the main gate, with the drawbridge over the moat, as the

Gate of the Heavenly Noodles. The Great Dining Hall was known as the Hall of the Crystalized Ginger. The winding steps leading to the keep were called the Macaroni Staircase. The long, flagged walk, where kings and queens had paced and pondered, became the Terrace of Tittering Toffy. And so on.

"Well, to get back to the Grand Picnic:

"Delicious dishes decked the length and breadth of hillside, heath, and meadow—acres and acres of elegant eating. Most of them were fancy things that had rarely been seen before, such as pickled samfire from the fenlands of Lincolnshire; mangoes sliced with strips of anchovy; curried prawns from Bombay powdered with dried ginger; lampreys steeped in nutmeg and old wine; grapes of Muscatel stuffed with cream cheese and powdered sugar; medlars pounded into a thick paste with pomegranate syrup; bamboo sprouts dressed with the juice of wild sloes. All these recipes, also, were set down with the most exact care in the great library of the Royal College of Cooking.

"Then there were the jamming and pickling competitions. Dame Gwendolyn Goosebury got the prize for jam, while Mistress Sourly Dill carried off the pickle honors. A special pavilion for children was set up. No one was put in charge; and sailing toy boats in the soup was permitted, and the diners let the chops fall where they may.

"Candies and sweetmeats were hung from the trees, and the King had even made the main stream into a River of Lemonade, from which the people—especially the youngsters—drank their fill. But this turned out, however, to be not altogether a success. The trout did not care for the lemon juice put into the river. It did not kill them nevertheless. It merely turned them into a new species. Instead of speckled trout, they became the far-famed *sour-faced trout*. And this most unusual fish was considered a great delicacy from that time on.

"Then there were food games and gambols—such as the potato race, ducking for apples in the tub, tossing the pancake, etc.

"But the most important feature of the Picnic was the prize given for a new vegetable. The Marchioness of Cling and Cloy brought out an edible rose—a tea rose that could be used in place of camomile or coffee. And everyone thought she would surely win the prize. But the judges declared this was not truly a vegetable, and therefore the Marchioness's rose could not be considered. However, Squire Squab, who had spent much time in his vegetable garden, produced something which no one had ever heard of before—a cross between a leek and a sea kale. This caused quite a sensation, and the judges felt sure that the seeds of this unusual vegetable would turn out the prize winner.

"And Squire Squab was a very proud man."

THE TENTH AND LAST EVENING

HOW PRINCE NASTIBOZO, THE KING'S OWN
NEPHEW, PLOTTED TO OVERTHROW HIS WELL-
BELOVED UNCLE AND REIGN IN HIS STEAD.
REVOLUTION IS BROUGHT UPON THE LAND
THROUGH THE WICKEDNESS OF THE
CHANCELLOR OF THE EXCHEQUER.
GUZZLE THE SECOND IS EXILED.
THE COUNTERREVOLUTIONISTS THROW
OUT NASTIBOZO AND TRY TO BRING BACK
THE OLD KING TO THE THRONE. THE GOLDEN
SAUCEPAN AND THE "PICNIC KING'S" LAST
PROMISE TO HIS PEOPLE

"But at this point in my story I have to bring in a
very unscrupulous villain, no other than Prince Nasti-

bozo, the King's own nephew. This man, without conscience and without shame, had been in partnership for some time with another rogue, but one of a very different kind. He was the Chancellor of the Exchequer and his job was to see to the expenses of the palace and the royal living. He had a very bad digestion, had the Chancellor — so bad that a mere custard or the lightest soufflé could give him a violent stomachache.

"This did not improve his disposition, which was bad enough already. He was very much against the King's spending money for food — which he couldn't eat — and especially against the new Vegetable Competition and the whole of the Grand Picnic. Therefore when Prince Nastibozo came to him with a wicked plan, the Chancellor of the Exchequer was very pleased.

"You must understand that the seeds of Squire Squab's new vegetable were as yet very scarce and very hard to get. There were only four in existence, and the Squire, in order to make sure of a good plant to show the judges, intended to plant them all. He was a real sportsman, and if no good plant came up from all four seeds, he would take his loss and misfortune like the gentleman he was.

"So when Prince Nastibozo came to the Chancellor of the Exchequer and told him he knew where the seeds were hidden, the Chancellor shook with fiendish laughter — in spite of having a bad stomachache at that very moment. For he saw at once that if Nastibozo only poisoned the seeds with acid, no good plant could possibly grow up for the judges to consider. Chuckling with glee, the Chancellor complimented Nastibozo as a clever prince, worthy in all things of his uncle's throne, that someday before long must be left empty.

"You see, there was double wickedness in the black heart of the Chancellor. He hoped, as we say, to kill two birds with one stone. Not only would he beat the worthy Squire Squab of Squelchley-on-the-Squeam, but he trusted he would do something more important as well. For years he had been going to the doctors with insides desperately upset by the rich dishes devised by his master, the 'Picnic King.' Moreover, he did not by any means approve of spending the country's great wealth in such frivolous ways. He hated King Guzzle the Second. And would have been glad to see anyone take his place.

"Here, then, was a grand chance for a revolution. Guzzledom in those days was an Elective Kingdom — that is, a king's son did not necessarily follow him.

But the new monarch was chosen by the people, and if troublous times came along, you never knew who might rule the country.

"Now, at last, the wicked Chancellor saw his Star of Hope rising. Everything was right—and ripe—for the overthrow of King Guzzle the Second. Even though that monarch had changed his ways somewhat of late, the people could still be told that the greater part of the country's money was spent in food and extravagant living; the brave days of Guzzle the First deserved to be brought back.

"Nastibozo was an important prince with a big following. Even if the people did not cry out for a new king, a revolution could be arranged, the Chancellor was sure. All he had to do was to send messengers to those foreign countries who had lent money to the Picnic Kingdom, and tell them all to insist that their loans be returned to them next Monday noon and not an instant later.

"This would be sure to throw all the business of Guzzledom into a great mess, and almost certainly cause a revolution. For anyone to find money in a hurry to pay his debts with is always difficult, but with regular merchants it gets them so worked up they are ready to do almost anything.

"And so there was a revolution in Guzzledom—the

first and the only one in that Kingdom's history. People ran around in all directions, did a great deal of talking, and acted in a perfectly crazy manner. The King's nephew, Prince Nastibozo, aided by the Chancellor, was busy as a bee, everywhere plotting and stirring up hatred against the King and the King's friends. There were many shootings and blowing up of public buildings. Nobody seemed to know quite what he was doing, or what might happen any minute. Business came to a dead stop. Shops were closed. It was a terrible mess.

"All this saddened the heart of the good King. It was not that he was afraid of Prince Nastibozo and his other enemies; it was not that he was greatly worried about the danger of losing his power as monarch. But after years of kingship he had come to think of the people always as his children. And now to find that they would turn against him just because a stupid popinjay like Nastibozo had done a lot of lowdown gossip and backbiting was something very bitter and hard for an old man to bear. It must not be forgotten that His Majesty was no longer a young man.

"He felt pretty sure that by fighting his nephew, he could beat him. But this he did not want to do. It would mean retraining the army and calling to his help all the noblemen of the countryside with their men-at-arms and archers. Thus, most likely, he would stay on as king. But before he could be victorious over his enemies he knew he would have to spread the horrors of war over his beloved land—a war in which many innocent people would suffer and be killed, just because they had been silly enough to listen to Nastibozo and his lies.

" 'No,' said the King. 'Whatever happens, there shall be no war. I spent my days teaching the people what are the good things of life and peace: shall I end my days by shooting them like dogs? No!'

"This his nephew and the Chancellor felt quite sure would be the King's decision. Guzzledom had been for many years a country of farming, stock raising, and the sensible, useful arts. The Chancellor knew right well that by getting the foreign powers to call their loans the Kingdom was not really made the poorer at all. It only gave the appearance of this; and the whole world believed hard times were now coming to every land upon the earth because the richest of them all seemed suddenly to have gone poor.

"Nastibozo and the Chancellor took advantage of this also. They told the people that great poverty had come upon them because the arts of war had been neglected. The cure for this, they said, was to make the country what is called an industrial one. Factories must be built everywhere—never mind about the farms—they needed especially the kind of factory that made swords and armor and cannon and those other things that are used for fighting.

"Thus they persuaded the poor, ignorant people that evil days had justly come to Guzzledom because the arts of war—by which the King's brave father, Guzzle the First, had made his reign so rich in victories and successful campaigns—had been laid aside and forgotten.

"Their idea also was to prepare for a revolution against the King that was sure to bring them success—when Prince Nastibozo was to grasp the crown and the Chancellor be made his Prime Minister.

"Clever in politics, these two.

"And at first they succeeded. Such was the terrible confusion that came over the peaceful land, nobody knew which party to join, and the King was nearly killed more than once. But quiet, kindly old gentleman that he was, Guzzle the Second was above all things a brave man. And where many monarchs in like position would have hidden themselves in the cellar or fled from the city, he walked the streets without even a guard.

" 'My children'—as he always called the common people—'will do me no harm,' said he to the anxious ministers who wanted him to stay indoors when guns were going off in all directions. This had the effect of making the people, who had always liked him, think it would be a good idea to keep him as king instead of setting up Prince Nastibozo, whom, for all his clever talk, they disliked and suspected without knowing why.

"Thus the country was sadly divided. The wealthy merchants and the army were all for Prince Nastibozo. So were some of the more powerful nobles, dukes, and the like. But the common people, the country gentlemen and the farmers, they were solidly for the King. And certain they were that given a proper chance, he would bring back good times and make Guzzledom once more the richest land in all the world.

"And so to decide what should be done about the matter, a kind of meeting was held. The King was put on trial. It was a tremendous affair. Nastibozo came with the wicked Chancellor, and both of them talked themselves blue in the face. They hoped that if they could only make things look black enough for the

King, they'd get the judges to order his head chopped off and then everything would be easy.

"But this the judges would not consent to do. Even if they had wanted it, they were afraid of the people. However, Nastibozo and the Chancellor made some very clever arguments, and after six hours of talk it was decided that His Majesty's life should be spared but he should be sentenced to exile — that is, he must leave the country and give up being king. Prince Nastibozo was elected in his place to rule the land.

"And so Guzzle the Second packed up his trunks and with a few servants and a dog or two he set off for a foreign country, while King Nastibozo settled down to be monarch in his place.

"But after a week he found that the business of being a king was not so easy. For one thing, he was not popular at all. As soon as the people had time to become quiet and could think straight, they made up their minds that the last thing in the world they wanted was a lot of factories to make swords and armor and guns. They straightway set fire to these and burned them to the ground.

"King Nastibozo turned the soldiers on them and many were killed and wounded. Then it leaked out that the wicked Chancellor had asked the foreign merchants to call the debts, and this made everybody perfectly furious. In the middle of the night two hundred farmers called on Nastibozo and told him to get out of Guzzledom before daybreak and take the Chancellor and his bad digestion with him.

"By daybreak they were gone and were never seen in Guzzledom again. Thus the Kingdom was left without a king. And there followed what is called a counterrevolution—that is, a new lot of rebels set to work to undo what had been done by the first lot. The army was dismissed and put to digging potatoes.

"Then there was much discussion whether they should try to get King Guzzle the Second to come back. The counterrevolutionists won easily. And the same two hundred farmers set off to find him and bring him back.

"Well, they found him after a good deal of search in foreign lands, but they couldn't bring him back. He didn't want to come. He gave them several reasons; for one thing, he said, he was probably too old now to make a good king; for another, he was a little disappointed in the people of Guzzledom. The country would perhaps do better as a republic than as a kingdom.

"Finally he told them that the task he had set out to

do was done—he had taught his people the true value of the things worth while in living. He wanted now, he said, to settle down as a country gentleman to breed trout, to raise pheasants, and prune peach trees. And besides, as one of his dogs was going to have puppies in a few days, he couldn't possibly be absent for that, even for the ruling of a kingdom. Let them try a republic, he said, and see how it worked out.

"The farmers were very disappointed. But before they left they made him promise that once a year he would visit his old Kingdom to celebrate the Anniversary of Steak-and-Kidney Pudding. The famous Golden Saucepan, which he had so often used in years gone by, would be kept glittering and bright against his coming, and the silk apron he always wore in the royal kitchen would be specially laundered. He could not refuse this, they said, wiping their tears on red handkerchiefs—republic or no republic. He could come as a private gentleman visiting the state.

"This he swore solemnly he would do, insisting only that he bring his own dough with him—since the old pastry cook, the only one who could knead it to his taste—had refused to be left behind and had come to share his exile with him."

ABOUT THE AUTHOR

Hugh Lofting was born in England in 1886, and studied engineering in London and at the Massachusetts Institute of Technology. He settled in the United States after his marriage in 1912.

During World War I he was commissioned a lieutenant in the Irish Guards. Distressed by the suffering inflicted on animals by the war, he took up writing humorous illustrated letters to his children, and these eventually became *The Story of Doctor Dolittle*.

Hugh Lofting went on to write many other books for children, including *The Voyages of Doctor Doolittle,* which won the Newbery Medal in 1923. He died in California in 1947.